River Run

River Run Series

Book One
By M.L. Bullock

Table of Contents

Chapter One—Sophia

Chapter Two—Sophia

Chapter Three—Evie

Chapter Four—Mary Sanford—1658

Chapter Five—Sophia

Chapter Six—Mary

Chapter Seven—Sophia

Chapter Eight—Evie

Chapter Nine—Mary

Chapter Ten—Sophia

Chapter Eleven—Mary

Chapter Twelve—Sophia

Chapter Thirteen—Mary

Chapter Fourteen—Sophia

Chapter Fifteen—Sophia

Chapter Sixteen—Sophia

Epilogue—Sophia

Author's Note

Chapter One—Sophia

The sign loomed before us, old and weathered, standing like a sentinel at the edge of the property. It creaked slightly in the wind as it hung precariously from a rusty iron bar. "River Run," it read, the painted letters chipped and fading yet still proudly announcing our new home.

I would later look back on this moment and wonder why I hadn't sensed that this was a haunted place. A place of darkness and mystery.

My eyes widened as I gazed upon the grand estate of River Run for the first time. Thus far, I'd been relying on Mike's assurances. *Talk about a trust exercise. I can't believe I went along with this. Take that, Dr. McClure.*

Therapy had been Mike's idea, but Dr. McClure was the world's most pessimistic marriage counselor—or therapist, as he liked to be called. I was glad to be rid of him.

I shared an uneasy smile with my husband as we continued to make our way up the drive. Mike was the kind of guy that believed Hawaiian shirts were dressy. I mean, I'd seen pictures, but the photos didn't do this place justice. For once in his life, Mike hit the jackpot.

This was love at first sight. River Run made my spooky heart leap for joy. Yet, at that time, I didn't know the difference between spooky and evil. They weren't the same thing at all.

Nestled on the outskirts of Fairfield, Connecticut, the ancient house stood majestic yet somewhat forlorn, an architectural gem covered in creeping ivy and the shadows of its past. The roof's slate tiles bore the patina of age, and the windows seemed to hold back secrets and reflected the darkening sky's ever-changing moods.

A cold wind whispered through the ancient oaks that lined the property, their gnarled branches reaching out like twisted hands. Flocks of crows cawed ominously, their dark silhouettes cutting across the gray sky. The rustling of leaves and the distant rumble of thunder added to the eerie atmosphere.

"Mommy," my daughter Evie whined from the backseat. "Is this it?"

"I can't believe it's ours," I breathed, my voice trembling with excitement as I stared at the ornate iron gate, imagining the feel of the cold, time-worn metal under my fingertips. "It's like something out of a dream."

"More like a nightmare," I heard Evie whisper to herself. At least the boys weren't complaining yet. I shook my head in frustration. I began spouting off the distinct features of the house, the widow's walk, the gingerbread cutouts. It was an exercise in futility.

"Honey, it's an old house, but we'll make it ours," my husband promised our unhappy daughter. Mike, more matter of fact, squinted at the peeling paint and the slightly tilted chimney. "It does have a certain charm," he added, though his voice held a note of reservation. "I know this was my idea, but I hope it's not going to turn out to be a money pit."

I turned to him, my eyes sparkling with enthusiasm. Still, I was unable to shake a faint, inexplicable chill that danced down my spine. "Are you trying to jinx us? Mike, can't you feel it? The history, the mystery? It's perfect for us. Don't you think so, boys?"

The boys appeared excited, more about getting out of the van after six hours of almost nonstop driving than about anything else. Evie said nothing at all. My daughter didn't like change. The move and the new house would take some adjusting. It would be okay, though. At least I hoped it would.

Mike smiled, his eyes flickering with a hint of unease. "We'll make it perfect, together," he promised, though I caught his gaze roaming the property, foreseeing the work ahead and maybe something else. He paused for a moment, as if an indistinct shadow lurked at the corners of his perception.

As we made our way up the winding driveway to the front door, I felt a profound connection, as if the house had been waiting for us. River Run was a place where history lingered and shadows whispered of tragedies long past. It welcomed us with open arms, but in its dark corners and hidden recesses, something else stirred, waiting.

Waiting for me, waiting for all of us...

As Mike parked the van, my heart fluttered with a cocktail of anticipation, excitement, and apprehension. The scent of fresh earth, wildflowers, and the faint mustiness of an old, long-uninhabited house filled my nostrils. Our dream of owning a house with a bit of history was finally realized. This was a moment I never thought would come, but now it was here.

Mike, my ever-enthusiastic husband, was already unbuckling the youngest from the car seat, his eyes wide and bright as he took in the sprawling property. Noah was fast asleep still, so Mike held him.

"She's a beauty, but I hope she doesn't have any surprises in store for us. You know Grant and Rebecca took it in the pants when they bought their Victorian."

I smiled at him. "Hey, this was your idea, remember? Besides, you know Grant can't hit a nail with a hammer, much less renovate a Victorian home. You, my love, are far more talented." As expected, my husband practically beamed at hearing my compliments. But I had to agree that the old colonial-style house with its peeling paint and overgrown garden might cost us a dollar or two. Hopefully, it only cost us sweat equity and nothing else.

As I took my first step towards the house, I couldn't shake off the feeling that we were stepping into not just a new house but a new chapter of our lives, one that was going to change us in ways we could not even begin to fathom.

The imposing wooden front door of River Run loomed before us, a gateway to our new life. Its weathered surface bore intricate carvings that hinted at a time long past, and the old brass knocker seemed almost like an ancient sentinel guarding the secrets within.

Why on earth would I think like that? I'm not one to be macabre. Mike and I exchanged a playful glance as we stood at the threshold, each waiting for the other to take the lead. "Ladies first?" he offered, his voice teasing.

"Nonsense," I retorted with a mock sigh, pretending to be offended. "Since you're the handyman here, you should be the one to make sure the door doesn't fall off its hinges."

He chuckled, and the boys, Jamie and Noah, giggled, caught up in our banter. But Evie, our sensitive daughter and middle child, stood on the porch clutching her stuffed rabbit, her eyes wide and filled with apprehension. She nudged closer to me, and I welcomed her warmth.

"Come on, sweetheart," I coaxed, kneeling beside her. "Don't be afraid. It's just a new place. Don't you want to see your new room? I hear it has big windows."

"I don't like this place, Mommy," she whispered, her voice barely audible, her eyes never leaving the dark entrance. "It feels funny, and it makes my tummy wobbly."

"What do you mean?" I asked gently, trying to understand her fear. I wanted to sigh but refrained. Couldn't Evie just once face life without fear? My poor, fearful girl. Mike slid the key into the lock, and we all heard it click.

"It's...cold," she replied, her small voice trailing off, her expression distant. "And it's stinky."

"Stinky? It's musty, but I wouldn't say it was stinky. We must air it out and clean it up a bit." I hugged her tight, feeling a pang of sympathy for her unease. "It's a big change, honey, but we will be together. And I promise, once we fill it with our things, it'll feel warm and cozy. Maybe we should burn the pumpkin candle. That will make the house smell like pumpkin pie. That's your favorite. Right?"

I could feel her body relax slightly, but her eyes remained fixed on the open door, a shadow of uncertainty still lingering. Mike, now free of Noah, who was awake and ready to explore, must have sensed her discomfort. He lovingly reached down and swung her up into his arms.

"How about we explore it together? I bet there's a secret treasure hidden somewhere just waiting for you to find it. Probably gold and silver!" Evie's eyes sparkled at the mention of treasure, and she finally nodded, her grip on her stuffed rabbit loosening. I did my best not to feel jealous of the bond they had. I couldn't seem to connect with Evie, not like Mike could. Noah glanced up at him sadly. He'd changed his mind and wanted his father to carry him. But Mike patted his son's head and gently refused him. Noah clung to him regardless. He didn't like sharing his father with his sister, or anyone else. Usually, he was the one in Mike's arms.

Geesh, none of my kids were asking me to hold them. Well, at least my oldest and I seemed to have an unbreakable bond. There was comfort in that.

"For real, Dad? Pirates lived here?" That was Jamie, our oldest and most naïve of all the children. I winked at him to try to clue him in on the joke. He didn't seem to get it.

"Could be. Let's find out." With a triumphant smile, Mike pushed the heavy door the rest of the way open, and it creaked ominously, revealing the dark interior. The boys rushed past us, their youthful energy and excitement breaking through the momentary tension.

As we stepped into the dimly lit foyer, the smell of dust and age welcomed us. *Okay, Evie was right. It does smell a bit stinky.* The house was still and silent, as if holding its breath, waiting for us to enter fully.

The house seemed to beckon me forward, drawing me into its embrace. As I wandered through the first couple of rooms, I couldn't help but be enchanted by its character. Each room told a story, bearing the marks of time and history. The ornate moldings and creaking floorboards were all typical for the age of the house.

I can't believe I'm standing in a house originally built in the 1600s!

We found the living room. Its fireplace was adorned with carved wooden mantels, now cold and empty but hinting at the warmth it could provide. The walls were covered in faded wallpaper, its patterns intricate and mesmerizing. *Ugh. That will have to go. I hate peeling wallpaper. It takes forever.* Large bay windows overlooked the overgrown garden, letting in a muted, ethereal light.

"Mom, look at this!" Jamie called, pointing to a hidden compartment in a closet wall off the living area. Inside we found a collection of old books and letters, their edges yellowed and worn.

Mike's eyes sparkled as he picked up one of the letters, scanning its contents. "Seems like the previous owners were quite the writers," he said, his voice filled with intrigue. I wasn't too excited about some old letters—I had a house to explore. I could see the kitchen and had to go check it out. Mike handed the letters back to Jamie and followed me closely.

If we were going to lose money on this deal of a lifetime, it would be in the kitchen. Buying new appliances was out of the question, at least until next year. I opened the refrigerator. Thankfully, it was clean and operating just fine. I smiled at Mike and gave him a thumbs-up. The stove worked great too. It was a dated kitchen, but okay. I could work with this.

I took a deep breath, my senses coming alive as we began to explore the rest of the house. To our left, the dining room beckoned, its walls adorned with more faded wallpaper, the colors muted by time.

Majestic windows stretched from floor to ceiling, their heavy drapes bearing witness to countless sunrises and sunsets. "Wow, those dust catchers have to go," I muttered to myself. The second fireplace, grand and imposing, dominated one side, the wood above it stained from years of fires that had once warmed the room's inhabitants.

"Wow, look at this chandelier!" Mike exclaimed, drawing my attention upwards. True enough, a crystal chandelier hung majestically from the ceiling, its facets catching the dim light, casting a rainbow of colors. At least the ceiling was a bit higher in this room.

Quite a bit higher, actually.

"Nice. This room must have been added on later," I mused absently.

The boys, full of enthusiasm, rushed to the next room. It was a study of sorts. I trailed behind them. Dark wooden bookshelves lined the walls, filled with dusty tomes and forgotten stories. The scent of old paper and leather filled the room, reminding me of my grandmother's house. The study didn't capture Noah's imagination for long. He was climbing up the stairs, claiming his room, declaring it a pirate's den. Jamie continued to wander through the old parlor, his imagination ignited by the rows of dusty books.

My son, the bookworm. At least he wasn't staring at his phone or playing one of his many video games. I smiled at the sight of his curiosity.

"More books. This place is practically a library. Imagine leaving these books behind. Why would they do that?" Mike asked absently as he put Evie on the ground. Evie remained close to me, her eyes wide with curiosity but still holding on to her rabbit apprehensively.

As I watched Noah vanish, I caught a better view of the banisters. They were made of dark mahogany, carved with meticulous detail—vines, leaves, and even the occasional bird or butterfly. Every step he took on those stairs echoed through the halls, announcing his presence in this old dwelling. I decided to follow him, and so did the rest of the family.

The upstairs bedrooms held their charm. One room, perhaps Evie's future sanctuary, had a nook beside a window, perfect for a reading corner. The boys hadn't claimed it yet. I imagined her there in the nook, bathed in the golden light of the afternoon sun, engrossed in her fairy tales. I was happy to see her follow me and saunter over to the window seat and take a look.

Mike snuck up behind me and kissed my neck. I quickly kissed him back and hugged him.

"You did good, honey. It's a beautiful place."

"You think so?" he smiled down warmly. "Are you actually saying I picked out a good one?"

"Yes, I am." I kissed him again before pushing him away gently. I gave him a wink, as if to say, to be continued later. "Evie? Do you want to go outside and explore with me?" I didn't want to leave her alone yet. She was still apprehensive. I could read it on her face.

"Coming, Mommy!" Surprisingly, everyone wanted to go.

We headed to the backyard where the wild elegance of nature had reclaimed what once must have been a meticulously groomed garden. Stone paths, now nearly concealed under a thick carpet of moss and tendrils of creeping ivy, wound their way mysteriously through unruly beds of flowers. I wanted to follow each one of them.

Patches of color peeked through the greenery where defiant blossoms still thrust their heads towards the sun, their petals a testament to nature's persistence. Once upon a time, someone had planted flowers here, and the seeds remained and flourished.

Hmm...interesting.

In the center of this forgotten, unruly Eden stood an old stone fountain, its once-spraying waters now stilled by time. The basin was filled with rainwater, reflecting the cloud-dappled sky, and fronds of ferns draped gracefully over the stone, hinting at the grandeur it must have once possessed.

I could well imagine sculpted cherubs, worn by weather and age, frolicking around the fountain's edge, frozen in eternal playfulness. *Yes, it's almost like they belong there.*

Mike's eyes sparkled as he surveyed the overgrown scene, his imagination already transforming the wild tangle into a family oasis. "A bit of trimming here, some planting there, and this could be a real backyard paradise," he said, his voice tinged with the excitement of possibilities.

"Look, Mom!" Jamie's voice pulled me from my reverie, and he was pointing with wonder toward a grove of ancient trees at the property's edge. Amongst the dense foliage, a grand old apple tree proudly displayed its branches heavy with ripe, blushing fruit. The lush bounty seemed to beckon us, promising sweet memories in the making.

Noah was still clinging to his father's side. His voice was tinged with hope as he whispered, "Think there's a treehouse?"

Mike's wink was a pact sealed, his words a promise: "If there isn't, we'll build one, son."

The estate's age and the weight of its long history only added to the allure, weaving an intricate tapestry that seemed to envelop us. I felt an unexpected kinship with the house, as if the whispered tales of its past occupants resonated with our dreams and fears.

This was not merely a structure of wood and stone but a living entity, filled with quirks and creaks, secrets and stories, all beckoning us to write our unique chapter.

Standing there, amidst the tangled garden and beneath the watchful boughs of the ancient trees, I found myself whispering to Mike, my voice soft with the realization of a deep connection. "I think we're going to be very happy here."

His smile was warm, his eyes reflecting the myriad hues of the garden, his arm pulling me closer. "Together, we'll breathe life back into River Run," he vowed, his voice imbued with a blend of hope, determination, and love that promised to grow as wild and beautiful as the garden before us.

I can't say why, but I shivered.

Chapter Two—Sophia

The first few days in our new home were a tumultuous blend of exhilaration and exhaustion. As we unpacked boxes filled with cherished memories, the ancient hallways echoed with the boisterous laughter of our children, and rooms slowly transformed with familiar furniture and our favorite photographs. At times, I remember thinking it was as if we'd always been here. That River Run had always belonged to us.

Every creaking door, every window that refused to shut properly, and every old floorboard that groaned beneath our feet became a challenge we welcomed eagerly. Repairs were needed at every turn, and yet there was an undeniable joy in rolling up our sleeves and fixing our place.

Mike and I found ourselves delighting in the quirks of the house, teasing each other about the temperamental plumbing or the doors that seemed to have a mind of their own. If we shut one door in the upstairs hallway, another would open. Sometimes they all opened. We attributed the strangeness of the doors to old wood and the age of the house. Together, we turned these peculiarities into shared secrets.

It was as though the house, with its worn beauty and mysterious charm, wanted us to discover it and find one enchanting puzzle at a time.

Today's first major project was the kitchen sink, which seemed to take offense at our arrival by promptly developing a leak. It was a stubborn thing, the leak. It was as though the pipes were testing our resolve.

"There's a certain art to this," Mike announced, half his body lost under the sink, tools scattered around him like the remnants of a mechanical battlefield. I liked his positioning. I could study his flat stomach and lower half without him grinning at me.

Well, at least one of us managed to keep their figure. But then again, Mike hadn't given birth to four children.

My heart stirred at the memory of our lost child, my lost girl. We hadn't even named her. She was born and gone before I even got to see her. For a long time, I blamed Mike. Blamed him for not allowing me to have that moment to say goodbye. He said he wanted to save me from the emotional pain, but when I woke from the unexpected surgery, it all felt so surreal. The experience had broken the entire family's heart, and the children hardly understood death or that they would never meet their sister.

I was reminded of Dr. McClure's words to me: "Make the choice to forgive him, Sophia. He lost a daughter too."

I stood by the faucet with a wrench in hand, trying to match Mike's optimism. "It's a masterpiece, this plumbing," I teased, twisting the faucet and watching the water spray in an unexpected direction. "Damn!"

Mike's laughter echoed from beneath the sink, a warm sound that chased away the chill of the old house. *It was rather chilly in here this morning.* "I think that's it," he said, his voice filled with triumph. "Try it now, honey."

I turned the handle, holding my breath. For a moment, nothing happened. Then the water flowed smoothly, perfectly controlled. "We did it!" I exclaimed, my voice filled with relief and pride. In his excitement, Mike knocked his head against the piping and emerged with a grimace, rubbing the back of his head. But his eyes sparkled, and I couldn't help but laugh at his disheveled appearance.

"That's what you get for doubting the house," I chided playfully, helping him up.

He pulled me close, his hands damp but warm, his eyes mischievous. "I think the house and I have an understanding now." We kissed, a sweet, lingering kiss that tasted of victory and love. It was a perfect moment, a pause in the chaos of moving, a connection that seemed to root us to River Run—and each other.

That's when we heard it: a loud, unexplained stomping from upstairs. It was as though someone was marching back and forth in heavy boots. I broke away from the kiss, my heart pounding for a different reason now. "Jamie! Noah! Stop that racket!" I yelled, assuming it was the boys roughhousing.

Mike, still holding me, looked out the kitchen window. His face turned from confusion to alarm. "Sophia, the kids are outside." A chill raced down my spine as I followed his gaze. Sure enough, our children—all three of them—were playing in the yard, their laughter drifting through the open window. It was a lovely fall day, and I could hear the leaves crunching beneath their feet. I pulled away from him to get a better look. Sensing my panic, Mike tried to laugh it off, his voice forced and his smile not quite reaching his eyes. "Must be the ghost of River Run, playing tricks on us."

His words, meant as a joke, hung in the air like a dark cloud. A ghost? The idea seemed preposterous, yet the house's age and mysterious atmosphere lent itself to such thoughts. Suddenly, those whispered shadows, the odd creaks, and the chill in some rooms didn't feel so easily dismissed. I tilted my head to listen for further proof that someone may be upstairs, but there were no more footsteps. Nothing at all.

"Honey, I'm kidding. Hey, it's okay. It's an old house, Sophia. Don't go looking for ghosts." As he spoke, a strange sort of echo lingered on the word "ghosts," but Mike acted as though he heard nothing.

I tried to shake it off, but the excitement of the day turned into a heavy silence as we cleaned up, both lost in our thoughts. Mike's joke had unearthed something, a possibility that lurked in the corners of our minds. Was River Run truly haunted, or were we letting our imaginations run wild?

Only time would tell, but as night fell and the house settled into its nocturnal serenade of mysterious sounds, I couldn't shake the feeling that we were not alone here. River Run had welcomed us, but we were no longer alone.

*****

The warm glow of the dining room chandelier cast a golden hue over our first family dinner at River Run. Until tonight, we'd been eating sandwiches and pizza on the go. The table was set with mismatched dishes and silverware. Our fancier things were still packed away. Evie helped me arrange the silverware. *Sweet and thoughtful girl. I am sorry you will never meet your sister.* I pushed the thought away as we all gathered, our voices mingling with the comforting aroma of spaghetti sauce and garlic bread.

Despite her earlier excitement, Evie picked at her plate; her face scrunched up in that all-too-familiar look of disgust. "Mommy, there are tomatoes in this." Her saggy pigtails matched her unhappy expression perfectly.

Shoot. I forgot.

"I know, Evie," I replied, trying to keep the irritation out of my voice. "But we eat what's served in this house. You promised to try a bite. Remember?"

"But I hate tomatoes!" she protested, pushing her plate away. She poked out her bottom lip and turned up her nose at the plate before her.

Mike reached over, his voice gentle. "Sophia, maybe we can—"

"No, Mike. We can't." I cut him off, surprising even myself with the sharpness in my tone. "She needs to eat what's on her plate." I looked back at Evie, trying to soften my expression. "Just one bite, Evie. That's all I'm asking."

The room fell silent as Evie's eyes filled with tears. I could feel the weight of everyone's gaze, but I held my ground, even though I couldn't quite understand why this was making me so angry. *I did know she hated tomatoes. I knew and expected this. Why was I freaking out?* I was usually patient with Evie's quirks, but something was different tonight. Something was off.

Finally, with a trembling hand, Evie took a small bite. The relief in the room was palpable but short-lived. She gagged, spit it back out, and began to cry.

The joy of our first family dinner in our new home had been soured. "Boys, finish your food and get ready for bed. Evie, you can spit all you want. You're going to eat at least one bite." The boys quietly ate their meals and headed upstairs to get ready for bed. Mike refused to make eye contact with me and went to the living room to begin watching tonight's football game.

Nice. Thanks for the backup, buddy.

I began clearing the table, my mind a swirl of confusion and guilt. Evie poked at her food with her fork. Was she trying to piss me off or what?

"Evie, if you don't eat at least a bite, you won't help me make cookies tomorrow."

"But I don't like tomatoes, Mommy. I don't like them! They make me barf!"

I stared at her, but I was seeing red. Instead of arguing with my middle child, I slammed the soiled plates on the table, planning to get out of there before I screamed at my child.

Or worse.

Suddenly, the chandelier overhead caught my eye, and I paused, staring at it in disbelief. It was spinning, ever so slightly, and the crystals tinkled softly. The antique light fixture spun left and then right and then left again. Evie whined as she watched it with me. I walked to her chair and took her hand, easing her out of the seat.

"Mike," I called, my voice barely above a whisper. "Come look at this." I prayed he could hear me over his noisy television. "Evie, back away from the table."

He joined me, his eyes widening as too, noticed the strange phenomenon. "Must be a draft," he said, but his voice was uncertain. "Everyone step back. Might be the kids."

I shook my head, unable to shake a growing sense of unease. "There's no draft, Mike. The windows are all closed. The room above the dining room would be our room, wouldn't it?"

"Yeah, I guess you're right." We stood there, transfixed, as the chandelier continued its slow, ghostly dance, moving left and right. The odd movement cast eerie shadows across the room. Evie clutched me, our argument over dinner completely forgotten.

The house, with all its quirks and charm, had welcomed us. But at this moment, I couldn't help but wonder if we were still welcome. Had we awakened something else, something that lurked in the shadows, waiting?

"I'll go upstairs and see what those two are up to. You guys okay?" My husband's blue eyes searched mine.

"Yes, we're fine. I'll get started on the dishes. Look, it's slowing down. It's stopped now. Just like that."

After the dining room incident, we managed to finish cleaning up, each of us lost in our thoughts. Mike settled into the living room again with a tired frown. He quickly became engrossed in his football game. After washing the dishes and putting them away, I collected my daughter, who was parked by his side.

"Come on. Time for a bath. Jamie and Noah should be finished by now." She didn't argue with me, but she wasn't happy. Well, neither was I. The chandelier's mysterious dance still weighed on my mind, casting a shadow over the evening's events.

The boys seemed to sense the change in mood. Their laughter was a little more subdued, even though they hadn't seen the light dancing. I noticed their glances towards the darker corners of the house, their pauses at every odd noise. Even Evie's splashing in the bath was less exuberant than usual.

As I helped her into her pajamas, her innocent questions about the chandelier and the footsteps she'd heard us talking about earlier left me struggling for reassuring answers.

"It's just an old house, sweetie. Old houses make strange noises and do weird things sometimes," I told her, though my conviction was lacking. She looked up at me, her eyes wide and trusting, and I forced a smile, tucking a strand of her strawberry-blonde hair behind her oversized ear. Poor girl had her mother's ears.

"I'm sorry I don't like tomatoes, Mommy." Her large, expressive eyes were full of tears.

"It's okay, baby. Everything's fine. You'll see. We're going to have so many happy times here. I'll remember about the tomatoes next time."

Finally, she smiled back, the spark of her usual cheerfulness returning. "Stuffy likes the house, Mommy. He told me so."

"He did? Stuffy was always a smart rabbit."

The house had welcomed us, but it had also challenged us. And as I looked at my daughter, the memory of our lost child weighed again heavily on my heart. *Why? We'd lost her over a year ago. I thought I'd put these feelings behind me.*

River Run was supposed to be a new start, filled with hope and promise. I took a deep breath, ready to face the next challenge, ready to make this house our home, no matter what lay ahead.

"I shouldn't have lost my temper like that. I love you very much, and I am sorry." There. I needed to say it.

She looked at me, her eyes wide and shining, and then the tears began to flow. Both hers and mine. I pulled her into my arms, holding her close as she cried, feeling the weight of my mistake.

"It's okay, Mommy," she whispered, finally calming down. "I love you too."

We sat together for a few moments, the bond between us mending, and I tucked her in, kissing her forehead. "Sweet dreams, sweetheart."

Leaving her room, I flipped off the light and left the door open, just like she liked it. I made my way to check on Noah. I found him already asleep, his chest rising and falling in peaceful slumber. I couldn't help but smile at the sight of him, so content and innocent. So small for his age. He was a tiny version of Mike, whereas Jamie favored my father, tall and rather burly.

As I turned to leave, something caught my eye—a small shadow slipped behind the chifforobe. My shadow? My heart leaped into my throat, and I stared at the spot, unable to shake the eerie feeling that had settled over me. Surely, I was seeing things. I wanted to flick on the overhead light, but I didn't dare wake Noah, who didn't normally crash so quickly. It was only recently that he'd begun sleeping at night.

It's nothing. Probably a trick of the light or my imagination running wild. But the memory of the spinning chandelier and the unexplained stomping earlier lingered in my mind, filling me with a sense of dread.

Shaking off the unsettling thought, I headed to the master bathroom for a shower.

Mike's football game echoed up from the living room. His team was winning. That would certainly put him in a good mood. The noise reached me as I approached our bedroom, providing a comforting reminder of normality. I slipped into the bathroom, seeking solace in the routine of a warm shower. I quickly stripped down, dumped my clothes in the hamper and reached for a fresh towel. I hung it on the hook next to the shower and slid back the flimsy plastic curtain. I made a mental note to hang the fancy new shower curtain tomorrow. It was purple with a pretty fringe. It would certainly dress up the otherwise plain area.

The warm water felt soothing. I needed to wash away the tension of the day. *Thank God there is nothing wrong with the hot water heater.* I closed my eyes, letting the water cascade over me, feeling safe and relaxed. *Oof. That's too hot.*

I turned the knobs until I got the temperature where I wanted it. Oh, yes. Warm and even warmer. The hot water eased the tension in my muscles but not the unease in my mind. I reached for the shampoo, poured some into the palm of my hand, and rubbed it into my hair.

I needed a haircut soon. Mike liked my hair long, like how I wore it in high school, but I preferred something more manageable. Shoulder length seemed to be the perfect style for me. I liked my hair, but I could stand to shed a few pounds. Maybe some yard work would do me good. Those antidepressants had packed the pounds on me; I was glad to be off them at last.

I continued to soap up my hair and body and enjoyed feeling clean. I tucked my head under the spout and rinsed the shampoo away. As I turned back around to wash the soap from my face, an overwhelming sense of danger struck me.

That's when I felt it—a soft touch on my shoulder, like a caress. "Mike!" I sputtered with relief. His warm hand on my skin was a welcome surprise. It jolted me from my reverie, and I flung the water from my eyes with a smile, expecting to see Mike's teasing eyes staring back at me. But there was no one there.

The shower was empty, and a chill that had nothing to do with the temperature ran down my spine.

"Mike?" I called out, my voice trembling, the shower's steam turning suddenly oppressive. "That's not funny!" What kind of game was he playing?

Silence greeted me, and I quickly turned off the water, wrapping myself in my towel. The room felt different, charged with an unseen presence. I ignored my dripping hair and now-chattering teeth. Had the temperature dropped that quickly? The mirrors were fogged, but I could swear I saw a flicker of movement, a fleeting shadow that vanished as I looked directly at it.

Again? Why the hell am I seeing shadows?

I hurried to my bedroom and found Mike fast asleep in bed, oblivious to my panic. The game must have ended. My heart was still pounding as I tried to make sense of what had just happened. Was it my imagination, a trick of the tired mind, or had something truly touched me?

"Mike? Hey, Mike?"

He didn't answer but murmured as he turned his back to me and wallowed into his pillow. I quickly dried off my body and towel-dried my hair before putting on my pajamas.

I must be imagining this crap. What is wrong with me?

I clicked on the bedside lamp and glanced at my husband. No, he didn't stir a bit.

As I crawled into bed, pulling the covers tightly around me, I questioned our decision to move here. We were not alone here at River Run, and the night's embrace seemed to grow colder, filled with unknown possibilities.

I glanced one last time at the shadowed corners of the room, half-expecting to see something watching, waiting. But there was nothing—only the silence of a house that seemed to breathe with a life of its own and the lingering sensation of a touch that I could not explain.

The memory of the touch sickened me. Yes, something was amiss. River Run, with all its charm and quirks, had quickly become an unsettling place.

As I eventually drifted off to sleep, I couldn't escape the nagging worry that I was not alone. My sleep was filled with dreams and shadows, whispers of the past reaching out to me, beckoning me into the unknown. But I could catch none of them.

What else lay waiting for me, for all of us, in the shadows?

Chapter Three—Evie

It was a bright, sunny day, almost blindingly so. I squinted and wished I had sunglasses like Mommy. While Mommy and Daddy were lost in the rhythmic noise of cutting the grass and chopping up weeds, my brothers were trying to fly their paper planes, but it all looked very boring. I decided to wear my princess dress, the one with the frilly sleeves, and invited Stuffy, my favorite stuffed rabbit, to the garden for a tea party.

"Would you like some more tea, Stuffy?" I asked, pouring imaginary tea into his cup. I giggled as his button eyes seemed to twinkle in response. He was my closest friend, and I couldn't imagine spending a day without him. He sat obediently on the tree stump while I perched on my pink chair. Mommy had brought it downstairs for me, along with my table.

The garden was my favorite place. I hated the big, dark house with the squeaky sign in the front yard. Surrounded by pretty flowers and the warmth of sunlight, I felt the outside magic Mommy often talked about. A magic that could only be found in the sunshine. I was safe here.

I reached out to hand Stuffy a pretend cookie when I froze. In my bedroom window stood a girl, her appearance ghostly, her dress old and torn. Her long blonde hair seemed to float on an invisible breeze beside her. Was the fan on in my room?

No. The window to my room was open, but I hadn't opened it. I couldn't. I had tried before.

The sight of her hollow black eyes held me captive. "Hello!" I called shyly, waving too, but she just stared down at me. "Come down here!" I whispered, but her gaze never wavered.

What do I do?

"Stuffy, I think we have a new friend. Let's go say hello."

My heart pounded as I entered the house, and a sense of wrongness grew with each step. When I reached my bedroom door, a cold chill embraced me, making my skin crawl. The air was heavy, tainted with a fear I couldn't explain. Again, my stomach felt wobbly. I could very easily throw up, without any tomatoes.

Trembling, I slowly opened the door to chaos. I screamed at the sight. My room was destroyed, my bed mutilated, the stuffing pulled out like the insides of a wounded animal. My pink and yellow striped curtains were shredded, and my beloved stuffed animals and dolls lay decapitated, eyes missing, limbs torn off. Everything I loved had been ravaged by the horrible girl with the dark eyes. Who else could it be?

I clutched Stuffy closer. A scream clawed its way out of me. "Mommy! Mommy!" I cried, my voice breaking, my tears hot and unending. It didn't take long to hear Mommy and Daddy's footsteps running up the stairs.

"Evie, what happened? Oh my God!" Mommy shouted, pulling me into her arms. Her eyes widened as she looked at the window, the window where the little girl had been. But she was gone, and I never caught her.

"Mommy, look," I whispered fearfully, hanging on to her shirt and wishing with all my heart she would pick me up. But she wouldn't. She never picked me up anymore. Not since Baby Iris left. Nobody knew that I'd named the baby, but babies needed a name.

A silence, darker and deeper than the shadows in River Run, settled over us. "Why, Evie?" Mommy's voice trembled, and her eyes were filled with confusion I'd never seen before. "Why would you do this?"

"Come on, Sophia. No way she did this. She was just with us in the garden. I saw her come in two minutes ago. She'd have to be a ninja to do all this in that short of a time."

"I didn't, Mommy!" I sobbed, feeling a crushing weight in my chest. I could hardly believe Mommy thought me responsible for the destruction of all my things. "It was the girl in the window! She was there, Mommy! She was! I saw her! She had blonde hair and empty eyes!"

The boys raced up to join us. Jamie swore under his breath and whistled. As usual, he didn't get in trouble. He never got into trouble for anything. Not like me. Noah stood in the hallway, refusing to come inside the room.

"Who else could have done it? Ask your daughter, Michael! Why? Why would she do this?" Mommy snapped, her voice rising in anger. I'd never heard her sound this mad. "Look at what she's done! I can't believe this mess!" Mommy pulled away from me and picked up a handful of mattress stuffing.

Was this really happening? Maybe I was in a nightmare and I would wake up soon.

Please, God. Let me wake up soon.

"Evie wouldn't do this, Sophia," Daddy said, his voice firm but gentle. "How could she? Do you know the force it would take to flip a mattress and rip the stuffing out? Besides, we were all outside. I told you that. All three of the children were with us."

"But who else could've done it, Mike?" Mommy shouted, tears in her eyes. "The neighbors? Who would do this? We just bought her this bed!"

"Neighbors?" Jamie, my oldest brother, chimed in, his eyes wide with curiosity. "What neighbors? We don't have any."

Mommy's face went white, her mouth open, but no words came out. I cried because that's all I knew to do. I was terrified, and my heart was broken knowing that Mommy believed I would destroy my own bedroom. To my surprise, Mommy began to cry too.

Daddy put his arms around Mommy, trying to calm her. When it didn't work, he sighed. "I'll check the rest of the house," he said, looking determined but worried. "Everyone stay put."

He left the room, his steps echoing down the empty hallways of River Run. Jamie followed him, and Noah finally peeked inside the door, his face a mix of fascination and fear. He quickly left the room and left me and Mommy alone. I clung to Stuffy, my hands trembling.

At least I have you, Stuffy. At least I have you.

The room felt cold, even with the bright sun shining outside. The air was heavy with something dark and unspoken. River Run seemed to hold its breath, waiting. Waiting to scare us again. But where was the little girl?

Daddy returned, his face drawn and tired. "Nothing else is damaged," he reported, his voice almost a whisper. "Come on, honey. Let's go get a glass of soda. Soda for everyone." I took his hand, unsure who he was talking to when he said "Honey."

I didn't care as long as I got out of the room and away from Mommy.

Sitting around the kitchen table, glasses of soda half-filled and untouched, our family seemed caught in a hypnotic trance. I knew about hypnotic trances because Beezy, on my favorite cartoon, could use his eyes to put the bad guys in a hypnotic trance. Maybe that's what the girl did!

Daddy looked at me with a sort of seriousness I'd never seen in his eyes, a mixture of concern and puzzlement.

"Evie," he began, his voice gentle but probing, "I want you to tell me exactly what you saw when you came inside. Everything. From the beginning."

I stared into my soda; my reflection distorted by the bubbles. I felt lost and small and couldn't bear that Mommy wouldn't look at me. How could I explain something that no one would believe?

"Evie?" Daddy prompted, his hand on mine. "If you tell the truth, you have nothing to worry about."

Why did grownups tell lies like that? Lies were always better. They kept you from getting sent to your room.

I looked up, tears brimming in my eyes. I wanted to believe him, so I told him exactly what I saw. "I saw a girl, Daddy. In the window. She was there, looking at me. Watching me and Stuffy have a tea party. She had blonde hair, and her eyes were weird. I told her to come down, but she couldn't hear me. She had on a dress too. A princess dress, I think. I went upstairs to find her, and then she wasn't there anymore, but the room was all torn up, and everything was broken, and—"

My voice broke, and I buried my face in Stuffy. I had a lump in my throat, one that I could not swallow away.

Daddy's eyes met Mommy's, but she looked away, her expression distant and strained. She stood abruptly, leaving the table, and said, "I need to take my medicine."

Daddy's eyes lingered on her retreating figure before returning to me. "It's okay, Evie. You can sleep with me and Mommy tonight. We'll get your room tidied up tomorrow. What about you, boys? Did you see anyone coming into the house? Anyone on the property?"

"No, sir. We were flying the planes." Jamie answered as Noah nodded his head, wide-eyed.

"Evie, I know this is hard, but I need you to think. Could it have been a reflection that you saw? A shadow? Something that looked like a girl but wasn't?" His voice was calm and logical; he was trying to make sense of my terror.

"No, Daddy. It was a girl. A real girl. She had blonde hair and an old dress and..." I trailed off, knowing how unbelievable it all sounded.

He sighed, looking torn between wanting to believe me and needing to find a rational explanation. "We'll figure this out, honey. Don't worry about Mommy. She's just...we're both...it'll be alright, pumpkin."

But something had changed, something fundamental and profound. I knew that nothing would be alright. Jamie and Noah exchanged glances and then stared at me. We all had an unspoken, shared understanding that something had shifted in our family, something we couldn't quite grasp. Even they seemed unnerved by the events of the day.

"We'll put everything back together," Daddy said, more to himself than anyone else. "We'll make it right again."

But as night descended upon us, and the once-familiar shadows turned menacing, I couldn't shake the feeling that some things were broken beyond repair.

Would Mommy hate me forever for what happened in my room? Even if I didn't do it? That didn't seem fair at all.

Even though Daddy wanted to wait until tomorrow to fix my room, Mommy was having none of it. The rest of the day was a blur of cleaning and uneasy glances. Together, our family worked to restore my room, but it did not look the same. The air felt different, like the walls themselves were holding a grudge. Mommy barely spoke, her face pale, her eyes unfocused. Daddy's brow was furrowed, and he kept checking the locks on the doors and windows as if expecting an unwelcome guest.

Noah, never one to be brave, asked in a small voice if he could sleep with Jamie. Jamie rolled his eyes but agreed, his usual teasing tone absent. He was scared too, though he'd never admit it.

After dinner, Daddy called the police department, his voice filled with frustration like I'd never heard before. "No, I don't want to file an official report. I just thought you should know, in case there's been any other...incidents in the area." He hung up, looking more troubled than before. "Well, that's that. I don't know who else to call."

"We could call Uncle Pete. He's a minister," Mommy whispered as she rubbed his arm.

"We don't need a minister, Sophia. We need to keep the doors locked, is all."

The sun set, and the house grew quiet. Bathed and dressed for bed, I crawled into bed with Mommy and Daddy, clutching

Stuffy to my chest. But sleep was elusive. Every creak of the house, every rustle of the wind made me jump. Not just me, but Mommy too. Only she didn't hold me like she used to, and Daddy was asleep as fast as his head hit the pillow. I think all boys were like that.

When sleep finally claimed me, it brought me no peace. As I drifted off, I realized that I should have fought harder to stay awake. Should have tried harder...

I dreamed I was in the house, only the hallways were longer and more twisted, the darkness suffocating. The decorations were different too. There were no photographs of our family. No interesting knickknacks. Nothing but a corn husk doll and a few books on a lonely table upstairs.

I was running as fast as I could because I was being chased by the girl. Her voice was screaming in my ears, and her eyes were filled with a rage I couldn't understand. What had I done to deserve her hatred?

"Who are you?" I screamed back at her as I made yet another turn down the twisted hallway.

"Elizabeth," she hissed, her voice echoing in my ears. "My name is Elizabeth, and you need to leave this house. Leave this house or I will eat you! LEAVE THIS HOUSE!"

I woke with a scream, my heart pounding, my face wet with tears. Mommy and Daddy were at my side in an instant, their faces filled with concern. Yes, I was awake, but I didn't feel safe. I kept screaming. Screaming like my life depended on it.

"She's chasing me! She's going to get me! Mommy! Mommy! Help me!"

"Evie! Wake up! Honey! What's wrong, Evie? What is it?" Mommy asked, her voice trembling as she shook me awake.

That's when I became aware of the pain on my face. "My face! My face hurts! She ate my face!" I whimpered, touching my cheek. It was wet, and not with tears. My fingers came away red. "She bit me! She bit me!"

Daddy's face went as white as the sheets, and Mommy cried in horror. They stared at the deep scratch on my face, disbelief in their eyes. "Oh, God! Let me get the first aid kit. Stay right here, honey!"

Mommy disappeared for a moment while Daddy held me. I was shaking with fear. No, trembling. Inside and out. It was a horrible feeling. Like the kind of feeling you have when you think you're going to die.

"Baby, what happened?" Daddy asked as he examined my face. "Did you scratch yourself?"

"She...she did it. The girl with blonde hair. She was chasing me. She said I was in her home—that this was her house! She hates us—she hates me! She said she would eat me!"

"No more stories, Evie!" Mommy snapped, her voice filled with a wave of anger and fear like I'd never seen. "This has to stop!"

"Hey, Sophia! Calm down. Can't you see she's terrified?" Daddy pulled me close and slapped the last bandage on my face. "She didn't do this herself. She doesn't have any fingernails! Not the kind you'd need to slice your face."

"You're telling me a girl from her nightmare did this?" Mommy was picking up the pieces of her first aid kit angrily.

"But Mommy, it's real! Elizabeth is real! She wants me to leave her room! To leave her house!"

I sobbed, feeling terror that I couldn't put into words. The room grew cold, and for a moment, I thought I could hear the faintest whisper, a voice from a time long past, echoing my name.

That's when I realized the horrible truth. Stuffy was gone. "Mommy? Where is Stuffy?" I begged for her to help me, but she pretended to be asleep. Daddy was tired, but he flicked on the light and managed to help me search for my stuffed rabbit. Stuffy was nowhere to be found, and I knew who got him. Elizabeth had stolen Stuffy.

Chapter Four—Mary Sanford—1658

The lilacs were in bloom, their gentle fragrance filling the air and caressing my senses as I tended to our garden. River Run, the home Andrew's father had built and the place where we'd begun our life together, seemed to sing with the joy of spring. It was a humble dwelling, but it was ours, filled with love and the memories we were creating day by day. I tried not to show my pride; if the wrong person saw me too pleased with myself, that might invite trouble. Despite the beautiful day, trouble had arrived in Fairfield. There was no denying it.

Andrew was nearby, working on the wooden fence that marked the boundary of our property. His strong hands, covered with the marks of labor and care, were installing a new gate latch. I could hear the rhythmic sound of his hammer, a comforting reminder of his presence. Andrew grinned at me when he caught me staring.

"Mary, dear, what dost thou think of this?" he called, pointing to his handiwork.

I wiped my hands on my apron and pretended to study the fence latch—as if I weren't already watching every move he made. My heart fluttered at the sight of him, standing tall and proud, a smile in his eyes. "My heart, Andrew. Thou art a talented, strong man."

His face turned a shade redder, a boyish grin lighting up his features. "Well, if it's as perfect as thee, then will I know I have indeed done well."

We exchanged a glance, one filled with warmth and understanding. There were no words needed to express what we felt for each other. We were more than husband and wife; we were souls aflame, bound together by a love as deep as the river flowing near our home. It was a good thing no one else could hear us.

Our life at River Run was simple, guided by our Puritan beliefs. It was the only life I had ever known. Our small community of fellow Puritans was our sanctuary in a world that was growing increasingly hostile.

Last winter, there was talk about murders to the west. I felt sickened thinking about Seamus and Mary Worthy, the couple who had left our community for "greener pastures" and what Seamus called a freer way of living. The Worthy family was not openly denounced, but when word of their murders came to Fairfield, there were plenty of people that had something to say.

"Oh, that Seamus was always a wild man."

"The devil indeed lured them away."

"We must all stand firm in our ardent faith."

People said the mysterious people of these lands wanted to make war with us, but we had seen no evidence of that so far. Still, Andrew worked tirelessly on the fences, and we did our best to be prepared for whatever danger came our way.

Even more terrifying, we'd heard whispers of witch trials and terrible accusations of witchery, but in our haven, I felt safe from harm.

As the sun began to set, casting a golden glow over the landscape, Andrew and I sat on the porch, hands entwined. The world seemed to slow down, and all that mattered was the two of us and the love we shared. "Art thou hungry, husband? I have partridge pie left from this afternoon, and Rebecca gave us two apples. I will share one with thee."

"I would like that very much, but let us tarry here for a moment. The sun is setting. See the sunlight fading?"

I stared in the direction he pointed. I sighed as I laid my head on his shoulder. "I do see it, Andrew. Thou art always the romantic, are thou not?" I wanted to kiss him, but I would do no such thing. Such public displays of affection were forbidden, and decent people always kept control of themselves.

Yet, it was a thought of mine.

"With thee by my side, yes." He chuckled softly. I leaned against him, reassured by his strength and his love. But as the night closed in, a chill crept into the air, and I couldn't shake the feeling that the world was changing. Our home, our sanctuary, seemed to sigh as if burdened by a weight it couldn't bear.

Something was coming, something that would test our love, our faith, and our very existence. I always had a gentle knowing about such things. When bad things happened, I always heard their approach. Nightmares about death. Seeing black crows gathering in the trees outside my home. There were various ways to recognize the approach of bad luck and sad tidings. However, as a woman of faith I hid these things in my heart, never sharing them with anyone.

Oh, but verily I didst see a plenty of crows in the tree this evening. Their black eyes, full of foreboding, watched us most carefully. I feel it in my bones...ill tidings approach.

Please, O Lord, protect us. Keep evil from our doorstep and shield us in Thy grace.

At that moment, with Andrew by my side, I believed we could face anything. For we had each other, and we had River Run.

The day's labor, mixed with my unsettling premonitions, took its toll as the evening wore on. We moved inside, and I busied myself with preparing supper, warmed by the thought of sharing an apple and the partridge pie with Andrew. The scent of the pie filled the kitchen, a rich and comforting aroma that seemed to push away the darker thoughts for a moment.

"The kitchen of heaven cannot compare to thine, Mary!" Andrew said, coming up behind me and wrapping his arms around my waist.

I laughed, a bit of nervous energy escaping with the sound. "Husband! Shh. Do not speak so lowly of heaven's fare!"

Andrew kissed the top of my head, a simple and loving gesture that sent a profound wave of warmth and affection cascading through me. His lips lingered there for a moment, his breath soft against my skin, and I closed my eyes, momentarily lost in the bliss of our shared connection.

But as quickly as the contentment arrived, it was replaced by a sudden and overwhelming disorientation. The room began to spin, the edges of my vision blurring as a nauseating sensation welled up within me. The walls of our tidy home seemed to tilt and sway, the floor undulating beneath my feet. I reached out to steady myself, but my hand found only empty air.

The knife I had been holding, sharp and gleaming, slipped from my grasp. Time seemed to slow as it tumbled towards the floor, reflecting the flickering candlelight in strange and ominous patterns. I watched it fall, a dreadful sense of foreboding taking hold of me, a dark whisper in the recesses of my mind telling me that this was a portent, a sign of something more significant and more terrifying than a mere fainting spell. The knife clattered to the floor with a jarring noise that echoed through the room, a harsh and discordant sound that resonated with the fear building within me. Then, as suddenly as it had begun, the spinning stopped, and everything went dark.

I was consumed by a black void, an emptiness that was both terrifying and inexplicable.

I felt as if I were falling, tumbling through an endless abyss, my body weightless and my mind filled with images and sensations that I could not comprehend.

And then, nothing.

The silence was absolute, a profound and unsettling quiet that seemed to stretch on forever. I was adrift in a sea of darkness, lost and alone, a small and insignificant speck in a vast and uncaring universe. I knew, in that fleeting and terrifying moment before consciousness left me, that something had changed. Something had shifted within me, within us, within River Run.

A door had been opened, a threshold crossed, and there was no going back. The darkness claimed me, and I knew no more.

I awoke on the settee, Andrew's worried face hovering o'er me.

"Mary? Mary, my love, dost thou hear me?"

My head was pounding, but I managed to smile most feebly. "I am here, Andrew. What...what hath occurred?"

"You didst faint, dear heart. Right there in the kitchen," he said, his voice trembling. "Thou gavest me quite the fright."

I reached up to touch his face, reassuring myself that he was real, that we were safe. "I apologize, Andrew. I felt so faint all of a sudden."

His eyes widened as a thought struck him. "Mary, couldst thou be...?" He did not finish the sentence, but I knew what he meant. A smile spread across my face as I considered the possibility.

"With child? Oh, Andrew, dost thou think it so?" I had practically resigned myself to the impossibility of becoming a mother. Andrew and I had been wed for four years and there had been no sign. Could it be possible that we were now so blessed?

"It would be a blessing from the Lord, would it not?" His face lit up with joy, but there was a shadow in his eyes, a worry he could not quite hide.

"Yes, husband," I agreed, but my heart was heavy with the weight of my earlier premonitions. The crows, the foreboding feeling, the fainting spell—were they portents of something more wicked? Had this perceived come for the child in my womb? Was I now carrying our son or daughter?

We spent the evening in each other's arms, talking about the future and what it might hold. The idea of a child, a new life to nurture and love, filled us with hope and happiness. But as we lay in bed, the wind howling outside and the creaking of the house settling around us, I couldn't shake the feeling that something was lurking just beyond our reach.

Andrew sensed my unease and pulled me close. "We shall be well, Mary. We have our faith, we have each other, and we shall have our child. Naught can harm us here at River Run."

I wanted to believe him, wanted to trust that our love was strong enough to ward off any evil. But the crows in the trees, their black eyes watching, their caws a haunting reminder of the darkness, told a different story.

Something was coming, something that would challenge everything we held dear. And though we were filled with joy at the prospect of a child, I knew in my heart that we would be tested in ways we couldn't yet imagine. River Run, our sanctuary, our home, seemed to tremble with the secret knowledge of what lay ahead. It was as if the very walls were whispering a warning, a plea for us to prepare.

But for what, I couldn't say. Only time would reveal the truth. Until then, we had to hold on to each other, hold on to our faith, and pray that we would be strong enough to face whatever was coming our way.

The morning dawned, bright and clear, but the sense of foreboding that had settled over River Run refused to lift. The crows were still in the trees, their black eyes watching, unblinking and inscrutable—as if they knew something we did not.

It was in this uneasy atmosphere that Goody Ayres arrived, her face pale and drawn, her eyes filled with a mix of worry and fear. Her voice trembled as she explained her purpose.

"Mary, please, I beg thee. The child Elizabeth Kelly hath fallen ill, and quickly so. Thou art skilled with herbs and healing. Couldst thou help me? I need chickweed and anise hyssop, and quickly, for a healing tincture."

Her plea pulled at my heart, and I felt a surge of determination. I was needed, and I would not fail. I donned my white cap and apron, the fabric cool and crisp against my skin. I made my way to the garden with Goody Ayres trailing behind.

As I cut the chickweed and anise, the scent of the herbs mingling with the earthy aroma of freshly turned soil, Goody began to speak, her voice low and filled with concern.

"Thou hast heard the latest news, hast thou not?" she asked, glancing around as if fearing eavesdroppers. I wanted very much to stop her speaking, for I knew full well that her "news" would be nothing more than gossip. Gossip that would certainly terrify me.

"Verily, 'tis proclaimed that trials have commenced with solemn earnestness in Hartford. Tis spoken that both women and men stand accused of witchery, and that a number have been led to the gallows for such heinous transgressions. 'Tis told that the very air doth hang heavy with suspicion, that neighbor doth turn against neighbor, and that safety hath become a rare treasure. I ponder with a troubled heart what shall come to pass. Shall the devil make his way hither also?"

Her words sent a chill down my spine, and I found myself looking over my shoulder, half-expecting to see some lurking menace. The crows were still there, watching, always watching, their cawing a dark and ominous symphony that underscored Goody's words.

I shook my head, trying to clear it of the dark thoughts that had taken root. "Goody, we must not bend to fear and panic. We be righteous folk and follow the Lord's teachings. We have naught to fear from these trials. Refrain from speech of devils here."

But even as I spoke the words, I knew that they rang hollow. The world was changing, the ground shifting beneath our feet, and I could not escape the feeling that we were on the edge of a precipice, teetering betwixt salvation and damnation.

Goody looked at me, her eyes filled with a sense of sadness and understanding that went beyond words. "I hope thou art in the right, Mary. I hope thou art, indeed."

We continued our work in silence, the only sounds being the snip of my scissors and the cawing of the crows. Yes. The crows were a harbinger, a warning.

As I handed the herbs to Goody Ayres and watched her hurry away, her figure small and bent with worry, I made a silent prayer for the safety of Elizabeth Kelly and all of us.

Lightning cracked across the darkening sky. The air smelled of rain and dirt. The winds of change were blowing, and they carried with them a storm that would test us all.

Chapter Five—Sophia

Mike struggled with the closet door, and opening it seemed an impossible task. How on earth could the door have warped so severely overnight? I'd never seen such a thing. My husband attempted to laugh off my contemplation, saying that old doors warp from time to time. He wasn't fooling anyone. Certainly not me.

To make matters stranger, the sounds in the house were so...odd. The ticking of the mantelpiece clock sounded louder than ever before. Each cabinet door creaked when I opened it to replace a dish. Even the washing machine now made a strange swishing sound. Rather than bring that up to Mike, I left him to fight the door that kept some of our boxes hostage. It was as though the walls themselves were trying to tell me something, something urgent and terrifying.

Urgent and terrifying. Urgent and terrifying. Urgent and terrifying!

The phrase ran on repeat in my head.

The children, poor dears, seemed to be suffering too. At least they'd start school in a few days. Evie still woke up in the middle of the night, tears streaming down her face, claiming she had seen the ghostly Elizabeth standing at the foot of her bed. None of us could find Stuffy, which made matters even worse. Her face was healing, and she evidently had no scars.

The marks would still be visible for the beginning of school, but they were not red and infected.

Noah had begun to have nightmares too, nightmares that were too vivid, too real to be mere products of a child's imagination. Only our oldest, Jamie, appeared to be relatively untouched by the ghostly inhabitants of the house.

Mike pretended nothing was happening, even though he'd seen Evie's room and the chandelier and all the other disturbing crap. We'd sunk every dollar into River Run, as he reminded me daily, and we had to make this place work. No matter what. Still, while the kids and I were home alone and Mike was at work, strange things happened.

Toys moved on their own, books fell off shelves, doors slammed shut with no one near them. But it was never malicious, never harmful. It was like something—or someone—was trying to communicate, to reach out from the other side.

But for what purpose?

I tried to remain rational, so I agreed with Mike. I told myself that it was all in my head, that the stress and worry of recent events were playing tricks on me. But deep down, I knew that wasn't true. There was something here, something that wanted attention. My attention!

One evening, as I was tucking Evie into her new bed, she looked up at me, her big blue eyes filled with fear and confusion. I knew what she was thinking.

"I miss Stuffy too, sweetheart," I whispered, brushing her hair off her forehead and trying to ignore the lump in my throat.

Her eyes searched mine, looking for reassurance but finding only mirrored confusion. "Can we go back to our old home, Mommy? Please?"

"We can't, love. This is our home now." I forced a smile, but my words felt hollow even to my own ears. I kissed her goodnight and left her room, closing the door gently behind me. As I made my way down the hallway, I couldn't shake the feeling that I was being watched. The air seemed to have thickened, and each breath I took was labored. I felt as if I were smothering. I did my best not to panic and paused in front of the thermostat to check the temperature. It's not that it was hot. It was quite comfortable but hard to breathe.

Our youngest child, Noah, was already in the tub, his innocent face alight with joy, laughing and splashing about. The warm glow of the bathroom light seemed to dance on the water, creating sparkling reflections that filled the room with a golden haze. His playful glee was a balm to my frazzled nerves.

The house creaked around me, the walls themselves seeming to shift and bend, whispering secrets I couldn't decipher. I shook off my unease, focusing on Noah's happy face.

"Mommy!" Noah's delighted giggle pulled me back to the present, his small hands making waves in the water. "Look at me!"

I turned, smiling at his antics, but as I watched, something changed and rapidly. The room seemed to darken, the water in the tub rippling as if touched by an unseen hand. Noah's face contorted, his eyes widening in fear, his mouth opening in a soundless scream. He slipped, the water closing over him with an unnatural force, tendrils of liquid reaching up to pull him under.

What in God's name am I seeing?

I leaped forward, my heart in my throat, fear turning to ice in my veins. The tub seemed to twist, the water turning dark and endless. It became a gaping maw that threatened to swallow my son whole.

"Noah!" I screamed, my voice piercing through the cold silence of the house, ricocheting off the walls like a haunting echo. I reached into the water, grasping at him, pulling his small, limp, and cold body from the clutching embrace of the depths. The water writhed, clinging to him as if it had a will of its own, reluctant to relinquish its grip.

The room snapped back to normalcy, the water settling into a deceptive calm, the light bright and innocuous. But I could feel the shadows lingering, lurking in the corners, watching us with unseen eyes, waiting for their moment. Noah's frightened eyes met mine, filled with terror and confusion I could not ease. What had just happened? What unseen force had tried to claim him? A chilling hum vibrated through the house, a sound of satisfaction that sent shivers down my spine.

We were not alone. I reached for the towel and wrapped it around my shaking child's body. Something was here, something ancient and malevolent, awakened, and aware. It had noticed us and turned its malignant attention our way. Our new home, once filled with promise and hope, had become a place of terror, a maze of secrets and darkness that were slowly beginning to twist and writhe their way into our lives.

"Leave us alone! Leave my children alone!" I screamed at the empty air.

A cold wind seemed to whisper through the room, the shadows shifting as if in response.

The room spun around me as Mike burst in, his face ashen and eyes wild. Together, we bundled Noah in our trembling hands, trying to comfort him as best we could.

"What happened?" Mike's voice was a strained whisper, his eyes darting around the room, taking in the water that had spilled across the floor. "That's going to warp, you know."

"Mike, really? Noah got hurt! Something...grabbed him. I don't know," I stammered, my voice breaking as tears streamed down my face. "It's like something pulled him under." My words hung in the air, heavy and implausible. The house was alive, reaching out to us, but Mike's expression told me he couldn't—or wouldn't—believe it.

But I knew. I knew if things continued the way that they were, we wouldn't make it. The house wanted our children. The haunting reality settled over me: We were trapped in a nightmare, and it was only just beginning.

Everything went silent for a few days until at last, the children were off to school, their faces a mixture of excitement and trepidation. This would be Noah's first year, and I wanted to escort him to his kindergarten homeroom more than anything. However, the school asked parents to avoid personal drop-offs, and I decided not to embarrass my little boy by crying in the classroom doorway. Evie was proud to be a second grader, and Jamie barely spoke to me as I dropped him off.

"Goodbye, fifth grader! Have a great day." Jamie had gone quiet, sullen in the days since Noah's near drowning. Perhaps like me, he believed he might be next.

Mike had taken the day off, a rare event that both warmed my heart and worried my soul. Still, it was nice of him to be a part of the children's launch into a new school. I hated seeing the house as we drove up the winding drive. We would be alone in the house, and it felt as if the shadows of River Run grew longer as the days wore on. I wracked my brain for reasons to go to the farmer's market or the refurb furniture shop, but there wasn't money in the budget for splurges now. Not after plopping down a ton of money for school clothes and supplies. "I think I'll fix the old mantel clock," Mike announced, a determined look in his eyes. "And maybe the squeaky cabinets in the kitchen. They seem to get louder each day. Time to make hay while the sun shines. I don't know when I can take another day off."

I nodded, trying to shake off the ominous feeling that had settled in my chest. "You noticed that too?" I laughed, trying to sound playful, but I was glad it wasn't just me. I'd been listening to all sorts of strange sounds in this house. "That sounds wonderful, honey. Let me make us some brunch first."

We spent the morning in companionable silence. The house was oddly quiet without the children's laughter. I made Mike his favorite, bacon, lettuce, and tomato sandwiches. I quickly tidied up the kitchen and began cleaning. The more we worked, the more the sense of foreboding grew, a thickening fog that refused to lift.

Mike was having no luck with the mantel clock, an ancient piece that had started ticking the moment we moved in. It ticked, only its hands were frozen at 3:07, a time that seemed to taunt us with its insignificance. Or significance. Who could know? How could the clock tick without the hands moving? It was beyond me.

I was dusting the porcelain figures in the china cabinet when it began—a faint, otherworldly murmur, like whispers from the grave. My hands stilled, my ears straining to catch the distant sound. Then a sharp cry filled the air, filled with pain and terror. It was Mike's voice.

"Mike!" I screamed, dropping the duster. The floor seemed to shift beneath my feet, the air thickening with dread as I raced into the living room. "Mike! Can you hear that?"

What I saw froze my blood and made my heart stop dead in its tracks. Mike was suspended in midair, his body twisted and contorted in an unnatural arch, his face a mask of pure agony. His eyes met mine, filled with confusion and terror, a silent plea for help. His mouth was open in a silent scream, his body trembling.

"Holy God!" I screamed at the sight of my husband floating awkwardly in the air.

The mantel clock, a forgotten relic from a time long past, had come to life. Its hands spun wildly, the ticking growing louder and louder until it was a deafening roar, drowning out everything else. It was an otherworldly sound, filled with malice and rage, an angry heartbeat that resonated through the room.

"Help me, Sophia!" Mike gasped, his voice barely a whisper over the din of the clock. His eyes were wild, his face pale and drawn, beads of sweat running down his brow. He was moving higher by the second. What did this thing plan to do? Take him to the ceiling and then drop him?

"Mike! Oh God!" I lunged forward, reaching out to him, but an invisible force repelled me, sending me crashing to the floor. I cried out in pain, my body aching, but the terror was stronger, propelling me to my feet. "No! Mike!" I felt hands, small hands all over my body. They slapped and punched me, and I screamed in terror.

The room was alive, charged with malevolent energy. It was sickening, and I fought the urge to vomit. The air was thick, heavy, pressing down on me. Shadows danced across the walls, shapes moving in the corners of my eyes. Everything was twisted, distorted, a nightmarish reality that neither of us could escape.

"Let him go!" I screamed, tears streaming down my face. My voice was raw, filled with a terror I had never known. "Let him go, you bastards! In God's name—let him go!"

To my surprise, the invisible terror responded, the temperature dropping suddenly, a cold wind swirling around me. The clock's ticking reached a feverish pitch, a crescendo of madness that threatened to engulf us all.

With all my might, I screamed again. "Let us go!" And then, just as suddenly as it had begun, it stopped. Mike collapsed to the floor, the clock's hands returning to 3:07, the room falling into an unnatural silence.

I rushed to Mike's side, cradling his trembling body, tears of relief and terror mingling on my cheeks. "Mike! Mike? Honey, wake up! Please! Mike!" He moaned awake and suddenly grabbed me, holding me. We cried together, but at least we were alive.

The house had spoken, its message clear and terrifying. We were not alone. We were not safe.

The haunting had only just begun.

Chapter Six—Mary

In the early hours, before the sun had graced the sky with its gentle warmth, came a sudden and desperate pounding at our door. My heart leaped within my breast, filled with a nameless dread, as I hurried to answer. Andrew had gone to the fields already, and I was alone.

To my relief, my unexpected guest was Goody Ayres. But her face was pale and drawn, her eyes wild with terror. She fell upon me, her body shaking, her voice a desperate whisper.

"Mary, thou must help me!" she cried, her hands clutching at my arms. "The child Elizabeth Kelly hath worsened, and the Kelly family hath complained about my methods. There are whispers, Mary, whispers that I shall be accused of witchcraft!"

I felt a chill run down my spine, the words hanging heavy in the air. Witchcraft was a most serious charge, one that could lead to death. I was torn between turning my troubled friend away and comforting her.

"Fear not, Goody," I said, trying to console her, my voice steady despite the fear that gnawed at my insides. "Thou art a good and pious woman. None shall believe such wicked lies. Why wouldst the Kellys say such things? Surely you hear amiss." But even as I spoke the words, I knew that they rang hollow.

"Thou art a goodly woman, Mary Sanford. Speak to the Kellys on my behalf. It was only thy herbs did I use! I used no other!"

"Goody, please return home. I will speak to Andrew and then seek you out. Go now."

Even as she scurried back to her home, I feared the worst. The world was changing, suspicion and fear creeping into every heart. The moral ground shifted beneath our feet.

Why shouldst I be named? I had nothing at all to do with Goody's treatments!

Later that morning, Aimee Symon came to visit, bringing back my pie pan and offering some peaches. The news was not good. Not good for Goody Ayres at all. Little Elizabeth had died in horrible agony just this afternoon, her body wracked with pain, her eyes filled with terror. But it was the child's last words that struck the community to the core, her final accusation that sent a chill down my spine.

Aimee's pale face grew even paler as she repeated the bad news. "'She hath tormented me!' The child cried and wailed those words." Aimee's voice dropped to a hoarse whisper. "'Goody Ayres, she hath tormented me with witchcraft,' said she! The Kellys will demand a trial!"

The words echoed in my ears, a haunting refrain that I could not escape. I looked at Aimee, her face pale, her eyes filled with a sadness and understanding that went beyond words.

"I hope thou art wrong, Aimee," I said, my voice also barely a whisper. "I hope thou art wrong. I should go to Goody and comfort her."

"You should not do so, Mary Sanford. You should stay away from Goody and let her meet her own end." Aimee clutched my hand nervously. I could barely believe her coldness toward Goody, but had I not felt the same only this morning? But then she added, "Your name was also spoken, Mary."

I felt a chill run down my spine at Aimee's words, a cold foreboding settling in my soul. "Spoken by whom, Aimee? What art thou saying?"

Aimee's eyes were wide with fear, her lips trembling. "By the child, Elizabeth Kelly, before she was taken by the Lord. She did accuse Goody Ayres of tormenting her, and she did speak thy name as well. Thou must be careful, Mary. Rumors of witchcraft are spreading like wildfire through the village. I nah believe it, but others may take these words as truth."

I could scarce believe what I was hearing. My heart pounded in my chest; my hands grew cold. *Goody Ayres, accused of witchcraft? And my name spoken in connection with such a foul charge? What had I done save provide the needed herbs for salves and tinctures?*

"I have done nothing ill, Aimee Symon. Nothing at all, and Goody Ayres is a God-fearing woman," I protested, my voice rising in disbelief. "What have I done to warrant such an accusation? 'Tis madness!"

Aimee shook her head, tears welling in her eyes. "I know not, Mary, but the child's words have been taken to heart. Her family is distraught, and the village is in a panic. Thou must distance thyself from Goody and tread carefully. I fear that the whisperings and suspicions will only grow. God be with you, Mary."

Her words rang in my ears, a dire warning that I knew I could not ignore. The bonds of our small community were fraying, torn apart by fear and distrust. Where was my husband? What should I do?

I embraced Aimee, seeking comfort in her familiar presence, but I knew that things would never be the same again. We were teetering on the edge of a dark abyss, and I feared that we were about to be plunged into a nightmare from which there was no escape. She quickly fled, leaving me alone with my terror.

"Andrew!" I whispered as I left River Run and raced toward the field, the weight of the news heavy on my shoulders. I could not shake the feeling that something evil was at work, something far greater and more insidious than the mere ravings of a fevered child.

The lilacs were still in bloom, their gentle fragrance a cruel contrast to the storm that was gathering. Their beauty could not soothe my troubled soul. A time of reckoning was at hand, and I could only pray that the Lord would guide us through the darkness that lay ahead.

As I hastened towards the field where my beloved Andrew toiled, my mind was awhirl with the dreadful news. The very earth seemed to sense my distress, the smell of freshly turned soil reaching my nostrils, a scent both rich and grounding yet now tinged with a foreboding I could not shake.

The sight of Andrew, strong and steadfast, driving the oxen brought a fleeting comfort. He was a rock amid our turbulent times, a sanctuary I desperately needed. His brow glistened with honest sweat, his arms guiding the plow with practiced ease. The rhythmic movement of the oxen, their hooves trudging through the dark soil, seemed so ordinary, so at odds with the terror that gnawed at my insides.

"Andrew! I need thee!" I called, my voice cracking, my legs giving way as I reached him. I collapsed into his arms, overcome by a grief I could not yet fully comprehend.

"Mary, what ails thee?" he exclaimed, his face etched with concern as he held me close. "Why art thou so distressed? Is it the babe?"

I looked up at him, tears in my eyes, and the words tumbled out in a desperate rush. "No. Not the babe. Goody Ayres, Andrew. She hath been accused of witchcraft. The child Elizabeth Kelly hath died, and they say she accused Goody and—" I choked on the words, the fear in my heart threatening to overwhelm me.

"And what, Mary?" he urged, his eyes searching mine, his grip on me tightening.

"And me, Andrew. My name was spoken too. She says we cast witchcraft against her, but I have not touched the child," I whispered, the words a dreadful confirmation of my deepest fears. "I know not what to do, Andrew. We are on the edge of something dark and terrible, I fear. If only your father lived, he would not allow this evil to happen to me."

The late Mr. Sanford had been a judge and a good man, but since his death, our community had lost some of its dignity and decorum. Andrew pulled me close, his body a warm and solid presence. "Worry not. We shall face this together, Mary. Fear not. The truth will prevail. God will see us through."

I wanted to believe him. The smell of the earth, the sight of my beloved Andrew, the feel of his arms around me—all were now tinged with a terror that I could not escape.

The darkness was closing in, and I feared that neither faith nor love could save me from what lay ahead. At least I would not face it alone.

Chapter Seven—Sophia

The brush moved smoothly across the wall, its bristles leaving a trail of muted color as I worked to transform the dining room. *Was this color right? It was supposed to be a light sage green, but it looked more like a weird shade of mint. Ugh. Oh well. Too late now.*

Mike was at work, so I couldn't ask him for a second opinion. The kids were safely at school, and I had the whole house to myself—a rarity that I was relishing. Things had calmed down a bit since Mike's attack. I'd just about convinced myself I imagined it all, but that couldn't be true. Poor Noah remembered every detail of his encounter with the invisible, and now I had to sit in the bathroom with him while he took a shower. No more baths for my poor kindergartner.

My husband didn't want to talk about any of it. I know it terrified him, but he'd rather pretend nothing happened. He wasn't fooling me one bit. I knew he was terrified. But just for today, I pushed the memory away. I was angry. Not at Mike. Not at anyone but the damn ghost. I made up my mind that from this day forward, I would fight back. In my own way and in ways that were not blatantly challenging.

I would make River Run my own. I would make it ours.

The soothing sound of the radio filled the room, playing a soft melody that made me sway as I painted. Music from the 1970s was so underappreciated, in my opinion. I loved folk music but couldn't enjoy it with Mike around. He held no love for Captain and Tenille or Helen Reddy. For Mike, it had to be Bad Company or some other classic rock group.

My mind drifted, thoughts dancing in time with the music. It was a perfect day, or at least, it should have been. A sudden creaking upstairs cut through my reverie. I paused, brush in hand, and listened. The house was old, full of noises and groans, but this was different. It sounded like footsteps—again. I knew this sound all too well.

My heart began to pound in my chest as I turned an ear up to the ceiling. I set the paintbrush down, wiping my hands on a rag.

Stomp, stomp, stomp. Yes, someone was up there. *Calm down, Sophia. It's just the house settling.*

But the feeling in my gut told me otherwise. I made my way to the staircase, each step a reluctant movement towards the unknown. The footsteps continued, deliberate and slow, echoing through the empty hallways. I could feel a chill creeping up my spine, the air growing thick with tension. As I reached the top of the stairs, my breath caught in my throat.

The hallway was empty, but the footsteps continued, moving around—inside my bedroom. I followed, my body moving almost against my will, drawn by a force I couldn't explain.

As I neared the bedroom, the footsteps stopped. *Shit! Holy hell!* I screamed internally. *What am I doing?* I hesitated, my hand on the doorknob, uncertainty and fear warring within me. The door creaked open with a gentle turn of the knob, and I stepped inside.

The room was just as we had left it this morning, untouched since I'd climbed out to get the kids off to school. I'd neglected to make any of the beds thus far, but there was plenty of day ahead of me. But something was off, besides the tangled sheets and Mike's socks piled up at the foot of the bed. The air was charged, the very atmosphere alive with energy. My skin tingled, and my breath came in ragged gasps.

And then I saw her.

She stood by the window, her back to me, her figure illuminated by the pale light. Her long dark hair cascaded down her back, her dress simple yet elegant. She was as real as anything I had ever seen, and yet I knew that she wasn't truly there.

I couldn't move, couldn't speak.

What do I do? What do I do now? Scream? Cry? Talk to it? The longer I stared at it, the more crazed my questions were. One thing was for certain. I was not looking at a real-life woman.

To my horror, I could only watch as she slowly turned, her black eyes meeting mine. Those eyes, although black and doll-like, were filled with sadness and despair. Emotions that transcended time and space. The dead woman's lips moved—oh yes, she was dead—but no sound came out. She reached out to me, but I stepped back, doing my best to avoid contact.

Then, like a flickering bulb, she fluttered in and out twice and then she was gone.

I stood there, frozen, my mind struggling to comprehend what I had just witnessed. The atmosphere in the room returned to normal, the charge in the air dissipating, leaving only the haunting memory of the woman's presence. I stumbled back, my legs weak, my heart racing. I knew then that there was no denying the connection between us, no ignoring the path that lay ahead.

I had seen a ghost. There was a ghost in my house. Not the blonde child that terrorized my daughter but a woman. A woman with dark hair and pale skin. She had reached out to me across the centuries, seeking help.

"Hello? Where did you go?" I waited for an answer, but none came. I backed out of the room and went to the front porch where I did my best to clear my head.

The rest of the day passed in a blur; the image of the woman never leaving my mind. I halfheartedly finished my paint job and eventually made the beds, except mine.

I decided not to tell Mike. Not yet. How could I? *"Hey, honey, I saw a ghost in our bedroom today. Please pass the salt."*

That was absurd. I couldn't even begin to wrap my head around what had happened, let alone expect him to. As scared as I had been in the moment, I wasn't scared about the woman. She needed help, she needed me.

The kids came home from school, and life carried on, but the image of the woman never left me. Her sadness, her desperation—it was etched into my mind, haunting my every thought. Strangely enough, a name came to my mind. Mary. Her name was Mary. How did I know that?

That evening, after dinner, I found myself drawn to the study. There were books and papers that came with the house, things that we'd never really taken the time to go through. Somewhere in there, I felt sure that there might be a clue to the identity of the woman I had seen.

The kids were engrossed in a movie, and Mike was tinkering in the garage; his old truck needed a new oil filter. I took the time to begin my research. The musty smell of old paper filled the air as I opened box after box, leafing through yellowed photographs, faded letters, and ancient documents.

The woman I saw was from a long time ago. Long before photographs were readily available. How on earth would I figure out who she was? I sipped my whiskey; I'd treated myself with a small glass this evening. Mike knew about it and thankfully said nothing to me. He had no need to worry, I would not overindulge. Not this time. I would need a bit of something before tackling this task and then getting the kids bathed and in their beds.

Hours slipped away as I lost myself in the history of the house, the people who had lived here, the lives they had led. Luckily for me, Mike took on the chore of getting the kids ready for bed. I kept at it for hours and then, just as I was about to give up, I found it—a painting, or rather, a copy of an original painting.

This was Mary Sanford. The Sanfords were the original owners of River Run. "It's her," I said to no one in particular. It was her. This was most certainly the woman I had seen, only in this picture of her old painting her dark hair was pulled back, her eyes filled with that same sadness I had seen in my vision. She had been a real person. She had lived here, in this very house.

"Mary? Is that you?"

A shiver ran down my spine as I stared at the image in the yellowed book, the reality of what I had experienced crashing down around me. I looked for more information, anything that could tell me about what had happened to her. Her name was Mary Sanford, wife of Andrew Sanford. Her father-in-law, the eminent Judge Thaddeus Sanford, had built this place and left it to his son.

Mary Sanford, I am listening.

I closed the book, carefully placing it on my desk. *Tomorrow I will go to the library. I will learn everything I can about the Sanfords and why Mary might be haunting River Run.* There was no going back now. The past had reached out, pulling me into its embrace, and I had to see it through to the end, no matter where it led.

I only hoped that I was strong enough to face what lay ahead.

Chapter Eight—Evie

"Why am I the only one who sees her? Can't you see the ghosts?" I whispered desperately, hoping to find a confidante in my brother. The walk to the bus stop wasn't long, and once we got on the bus, Jamie would pretend he didn't know either of us. Stupid big brothers. I glanced back at Jamie, who was trailing us. He didn't even look me in the eye.

It had been Jamie's idea to begin taking the bus. I did not think Mommy would allow that, but she did. I was kind of glad. I still struggled to believe that Mommy loved me. She had been so different since the evil girl tore up my room.

"I see the ghosts too, Evie," Noah said as he held up his posterboard. "I don't want to talk about it anymore." It was such a windy morning, I worried that his project poster would fly away. Again, poor kid. Who gets homework the first week of school?

"Noah don't see anything, except our sister acting crazy. What's that all about, Evie? What's wrong with you these days? Are you still mad at Mom?"

I just stared at Jamie, who had decided to join us. I couldn't believe he thought I was making this up or that I'd punish Mom for a mistake she made a long time ago. She didn't drink anymore. Mom certainly didn't drink and drive. I shook my head at him.

"Shut up, Jamie. I don't care if you don't believe me! Shut up!" Tears stung my eyes, but I refused to let them fall.

Exasperated, Jamie finally said, "Come on, Evie. We're going to be late for the bus."

But despite his hatefulness, Elizabeth wouldn't leave me alone. It was like she was mad at me for something, but I had no way of knowing what that might be. Jamie didn't understand the danger we were all in, and he didn't believe me. But I know what I saw, and I know what I felt.

The school day went by too quickly. Soon we were back home and walking up the drive to our haunted house. Yes, it was a haunted house. Nobody could convince me otherwise. But not a nice haunted house with Casper. This was a terrifying house with Spooky Elizabeth, the ghost who liked snapping her teeth at me.

Once we got home, I tried to talk to my brothers again. I needed Jamie on my side. Noah was too little to help, but maybe together Jamie and I could stop her. If we didn't, things were only going to get worse.

As always, Jamie was on his video game after school. School was easy for him—my big brother was so smart—so he didn't even need to study much. "Jamie, you've got to believe me!" I begged him, tears in my eyes. "She's real. Elizabeth is real, and she's mean to me all the time. She bites me! Look! Look at my arms!"

He rolled his eyes and continued to play his video game. "Evie, you're just imagining things. You probably did that yourself. Ghosts aren't real. You're making up stories again. Stop reading those stupid Goosepimple books!"

"You mean Goosebumps, idiot!" I stomped my foot at him.

"You're acting like a baby. Get lost." Jamie slid his headset on and tried to ignore me.

"No, I'm not! I'm not a baby and I'm not making this up!" I insisted, grabbing his arm. "She locked me in my closet, Jamie! I was stuck in there with her, and she was laughing at me."

He paused his game and looked at me, finally giving me his full attention. "What do you mean she locked you in the closet?"

I could feel my heart racing as I remembered the terrifying encounter. "I was putting away my toys, and I heard her laugh. When I turned around, she was there, right behind me. She had these cold, black eyes, and she pushed me into the closet. Then the door slammed shut, and I couldn't get out. I could hear her laughing outside. I was so scared, Jamie. I thought I was going to be stuck in there forever."

Jamie's eyes widened, and he put his hand on my shoulder. "Evie, that's impossible. Doors don't lock on their own. Maybe it just got stuck, and you panicked."

I shook my head, tears spilling down my cheeks. "No, Jamie! I know what I saw. I know what I felt. She was there. She was real."

He sighed and pulled me into a hug. I could barely believe he had any sympathy for me. "Okay, okay. I believe you saw something. But it was probably just your imagination playing tricks on you."

I pulled away, frustrated that he still didn't understand. "It wasn't my imagination, Jamie. She was there. And she's not going away. She wants something from me. I know it. What if she deads me, Jamie?" I could never bring myself to say the word "kills," but the facts were it did almost happen to me.

I had almost been killed and more than once. Mommy was sorry for the time she almost killed us, but Daddy said we could have been dead. Now Elizabeth wanted to dead me too, but not in the car, in my dreams and in my closet. I'd seen the angels when they'd surrounded the car while we waited for the ambulance people to save us.

Poor Mommy had passed out and wouldn't wake up and there were fires everywhere. I shivered at the memory. But I hadn't seen any angels these days. None showed up in my dreams.

Jamie looked at me for a long moment, his face serious. "What do you mean? Do you really think she wants to dead you, Evie?" I nodded slowly; my eyes large as goose eggs. I shivered as I answered him. "Evie, if anything happens again, you come and tell me right away. We'll figure it out together, okay?" I nodded again, feeling a little better, but I was still scared.

"You believe me, Jamie?" I rubbed at the latest bite mark. It didn't hurt much today, but she'd probably bite me again tonight.

"Yes, I believe you."

I hugged him and left him to play his game. Still, I kept my room door open and sat down at my desk to do my homework. I glanced back at the closet door, but it remained shut, luckily. I hated the closet. I hated my room. I missed Stuffy with all my heart.

Ever since we moved into this big, old house, I'd been scared. More scared than I'd ever been before. I knew my family saw things too, but so far, there had been no family meeting about it. I couldn't understand why we couldn't move. I hated this old house, and it stunk sometimes. Like the first day we moved in, it stunk really bad, but I was the only one that seemed to smell it. It smelled like one of the dead squirrels I found in the backyard from time to time.

I took out a piece of paper and decided to try to draw a picture of the ghost. Maybe if I could show my parents a picture, they would believe me. My hand trembled as I picked up the pencil, the images of Elizabeth's face still fresh in my mind. The blank paper before me seemed to taunt me, daring me to recreate what I had seen. My heart pounded in my ears, and I took a deep breath to steady myself.

Slowly, I began to draw. The lines were squiggly at first, but as I continued, the picture began to take shape. The eyes were the hardest to draw. Those cold, black eyes that had stared into my soul. I tried to capture their emptiness, their anger, but the more I worked on them, the more they seemed to come to life on the page.

I felt a chill run down my spine, and I looked around the room as if expecting Elizabeth to be watching me. The room was empty, but I couldn't shake the feeling that I was being watched.

"Mommy? Are you there?" It could be Mommy. Sometimes she peeked her head in my room. But Mommy didn't come out. Nobody did. I pressed on, determined to finish the drawing.

Elizabeth's hair was stringy and wild, framing a face that was both young and old at the same time. I couldn't explain that. Her mouth was twisted into a wicked smile, lips cracked and dry. I could almost hear her laughter as I added the finishing touches, the sound of her scary voice echoing in my head.

I leaned back and stared at the drawing, my hands still shaking. It was her. Elizabeth. I had captured her on paper, but now she seemed even more real, more present. The image stared back at me, those dark eyes seeming to follow me as I moved. I felt a wave of wobbly in my tummy, and I had to look away. The drawing was more than just a picture; it was a window into something dark and terrifying. Something that wanted to reach out and pull me in.

Why had I drawn this?

I knew I couldn't show this to Daddy, not yet. He wouldn't understand. He would think I was just being creative or that I was letting my imagination run wild. But I knew what I had seen, and I knew what I had drawn.

Instead, I put the drawing away, hiding it in the back of my sketchbook. I didn't want to look at it again, but I knew I would. I knew I would have to face Elizabeth again. She was never going to leave me alone. *Not until she deads me.*

The bad feeling stuck with me, long after I put away my pencils, crayons, and sketchbook. I couldn't shake the sense that something had changed, that I had crossed a line I couldn't uncross. Elizabeth was no longer just a ghost; she was a presence, a force that I had awakened. Somehow, but how?

I was more terrified than ever. She's a ghost! I didn't need a stupid Goosebumps book to tell me that! She's a little ghost girl but not a friendly ghost. She's mean. Really mean. She's been showing up more and more. At first, it was just glances—I could see her in windows from afar or out the corner of my eye. Now, I could walk into a room and if there was no one else around, she'd be standing there, staring at me.

One night, I awoke with a sharp, agonizing pain in my arm. It felt like a hard pinch, and I knew immediately that it was Elizabeth. My heart pounded in terror as I reached over to feel the spot. I dared not turn on the light, afraid of what I might see, but even in the darkness, I could feel the swollen lump forming—a big, purple bruise, throbbing with every beat of my heart.

I hid under the covers, tears streaming down my face, and prayed for morning to come.

Another time, as I reached under my bed for my shoes, something snapped at my finger. I yelped in pain and pulled my hand back to find a small, bleeding wound. It was a bite mark, and it had come from under my bed where nothing but darkness lay.

Mommy put a bandage on it, but she didn't believe me when I told her about Elizabeth. She said I must have snagged it on something, but I knew better. It was a warning, a message from the ghost that she could reach me whenever she wanted.

I was tired. So very tired. Sometimes I fell asleep at school. I even got into trouble for it. I couldn't sleep well, and when I did sleep, the dead girl always showed up in my dreams. Mommy and Daddy wouldn't let me sleep with them too much anymore.

My fear was constant, never letting up. Stuffy was still missing, my fluffy, soft rabbit with big blue eyes that always seemed to sparkle with kindness. I couldn't even remember life without him. Technically, I was a "big girl" who no longer needed a stuffed animal toy for comfort, but he'd been stolen. Stolen by an evil ghost. I had looked everywhere for him after he went missing, but he was gone.

That was, until one fateful day when he suddenly reappeared.

He was sitting on the windowsill in my room, staring at me with those once-comforting eyes. But something was horribly wrong. His soft fur was gone, and his friendly eyes were replaced by a cold, malevolent glare. His eyes, once filled with warmth and friendship, were now ice cold, mirroring the dark cruelty I had seen in Elizabeth's.

I reached out to touch him, but I recoiled as I felt evil emanating from him. Yes, Stuffy had changed. He was no longer my beloved toy but a twisted mockery of what he once was, now made evil by the ghost. She was evil!

Yes, his fur, once fluffy and soft, was now coarse and matted. His smile, once reassuring, was now a sneer, contorted into an expression of pure malevolence. And those eyes, those terrible blue eyes, seemed to follow me wherever I went, watching me, judging me, accusing me.

Had she buried him in the ground? Taken him to the grave with her?

I knew then that nothing in my life would ever be the same again. Elizabeth had made her mark, not just on me but on everything I loved. Mommy. Stuffy. Jamie. Everyone!

Evil Elizabeth had taken my innocence, my security, my comfort, and left me with nothing but fear and confusion. I sat on the floor and cried as I stared at what used to be Stuffy.

Eventually, I picked him up, but he felt wrong. Heavy and cold. I threw him across the room, but he landed right back on the windowsill, staring at me. I ran screaming from the room to report Stuffy's return to Mommy. Mommy said I was being dramatic, but I knew better. Stuffy had changed.

He moved when I was not looking. I saw him in different places, always staring at me. Places I didn't put him. He was always watching. In the end, Mommy took Stuffy and hid him in the attic. I was both sad and relieved that I couldn't see him anymore.

I started walking in my sleep.

Mommy and Daddy said it was because I was stressed, but I knew it was because of Elizabeth. She was doing something bad to me.

One night about a week after Stuffy returned, I woke up outside again. I was in the neighbor's field, and I was barefoot. The sky was purple above and was littered with fat, glistening stars. It was cold, and I was scared. I ran towards the road and as I ran, I realized I had Stuffy. He was in my hand.

I screamed as I ran, but I could not turn him loose—he wouldn't let me go!

My heart was pounding, and I was shaking as I looked down at Stuffy in my hand, his malevolent eyes staring back at me. How had he ended up with me? I had not seen him since Mommy took him to the attic. As I stood on the side of the road, I heard laughter. Elizabeth's laughter. It was faint, almost a whisper on the wind, but it was there, taunting me.

I stumbled back towards our house, tears streaming down my face. I could feel Elizabeth's presence growing stronger, her power over me increasing. I knew she was responsible for all of this, and I was helpless to stop her.

I reached our house and found the back door unlocked. I crept inside, hoping not to wake anyone. But as I made my way up to my room, I realized something was horribly wrong. I could hear voices, angry voices, and they were coming from my parents' room.

"Damn it, Sophia, I can't believe you left the door unlocked again!" Daddy was shouting. "What if something had happened to her? What if she'd gotten hurt or lost?"

"I didn't leave it unlocked, Mike!" Mommy was crying. "I swear I locked it before I went to bed. You know I would never do anything to put our children in danger."

Daddy snorted at her. "Really, Soph?" Didn't they know I'd just returned? Didn't they know how much danger I was in?

"You're going to throw that up in my face again, are you? You'll never forgive me, Mike. Never!"

"I didn't say that. But Evie's going through something, and I need to know that you're taking it seriously."

"I am taking it seriously, Mike. I know what you're insinuating, but it wasn't me! I wouldn't hurt my own child! But there's only so much I can do. I can't control what's happening to her. I don't know how to help her. Do you?"

The pain in Mommy's voice was almost too much to bear. I could hear the fear and frustration in both of their voices, and I knew they were at a loss as to how to help me.

I stumbled to my room, my mind reeling. Everything was falling apart, and it was all because of Elizabeth. She was tearing my family apart, turning us against each other, and there was nothing I could do to stop her.

I closed my door and looked around my room, feeling a wave of despair wash over me. At least Stuffy wasn't clinging to my hand anymore. I dropped him on the floor. My room, once my sanctuary, was now a place of terror and torment. I looked at the closet, the windowsill, and the bed where I'd been bitten, and I knew that there was no escaping her.

Elizabeth was everywhere, and she was growing stronger every day. Why bother fighting?

I crawled into bed, pulling the covers tightly around me, but there was no comfort to be found. I couldn't escape the feeling that I was being watched, that Elizabeth was there, waiting for me to fall asleep so she could strike again. I don't know how long I lay there, my mind racing, my body trembling, but eventually, exhaustion took over and I drifted into a fitful sleep. The following night, I dreamed of Elizabeth again. She was standing at the foot of my bed, her black eyes boring into mine, her twisted smile mocking me. She reached out, her cold fingers brushing against my skin, and I screamed, waking myself up.

I sat up, my heart pounding, my skin covered in a cold sweat. The room was dark and there was no sign of Elizabeth, but I knew she had been there. I could still feel the chill of her touch, the weight of her gaze. She was haunting me, even in my dreams, and I knew that there was no escape.

Days turned into weeks, and the torment continued.

Elizabeth's power grew stronger, her attacks more frequent and more terrifying. My family was falling apart, and I was helpless to stop it. I was trapped in a nightmare with no way out.

And then, one day, something changed.

I was sitting in my room, doing my homework, when I heard a noise. It was faint at first, almost like a whisper, but it grew louder, more insistent. I looked up, my heart pounding, and I saw her.

Elizabeth was standing in the doorway, her black eyes fixed on me, her twisted smile wider than ever. But this time, there was something different. Her eyes were no longer cold and empty; they were filled with a burning intensity, a hunger that I had never seen before.

She stepped forward, her movements slow and deliberate, like a zombie! I could feel the temperature in the room drop. The air was thick with her presence, and I could feel her power pulsing through me. I was frozen, unable to move, unable to speak, as she reached out to me. Her fingers were cold and bony, and they wrapped around my wrist, pulling me towards her.

I tried to resist, but I was powerless against her. She was too strong, too determined, and I knew that there was no escape. Elizabeth pulled me closer, her eyes boring into mine, her smile widening, and I could feel her breath on my skin, cold and foul. It was at that moment that I realized I wasn't in my bed anymore. I was on the road outside the house. A car came barreling toward me fast. The headlights were bright, and the horn was loud. It almost hit me, but somehow, I managed to jump out of the way. The car made a lot of noise, but it didn't stop.

I ran home, crying. Mommy and Daddy met me on the porch. Mommy was crying and Daddy was running down the street towards the car, but he would never catch up with him.

"Evie, you must never do this again. This is dangerous, Evie. What were you thinking?"

"But Mommy...I don't know how to stop her. Elizabeth wants to dead me. She's angry, and I don't know why. She was in my dream, and look...oh no! I have Stuffy again! How did I get Stuffy? I don't want him! Mommy!" I wailed as I pitched the stuffed animal to the ground. Daddy scooped me up and held me close.

Mommy snatched the toy away up, stomped around to the side of the house, and tossed it into the garbage can. I could hear the lid slam down before she reappeared looking scared and angry. Nobody said anything else. We shuffled inside and pretended nothing happened, as we almost always did.

Elizabeth was everywhere now. In my dreams, in the mirror, in the corner of my room. She was angry because she was dead, and she wanted to hurt me. Or worse still. Dead me.

The day after my sleepwalking encounter, I woke up on the couch to find scratches on my arms and legs. When I went to my room to get dressed for school, I discovered that all my toys were broken. My drawings were torn up—except the drawing of Elizabeth. And Stuffy was there, sitting on the windowsill, watching me with those evil eyes.

I didn't know what to do. I was scared all the time. I wanted to leave the house, but Mommy and Daddy said we can't and I'm only a kid. Yes, Elizabeth was mad at me, and I didn't know why. But I knew she wouldn't stop.

She wouldn't ever leave me alone. She had a new toy now. Me. Not Stuffy. I was her toy.

I hoped that she didn't take me to the grave, like she did Stuffy. I hoped I didn't become evil like Stuffy.

If she deads me...that will be the end of me.

Forever.

And no one would be able to help me. It didn't stop. Night after night, I'd end up outside walking in the dark with Stuffy in my hand. Each night, I'd wake up and look down at my hand and see that Stuffy was there.

As I stumbled back toward my house again, I could feel Elizabeth watching me. Her presence was like a chill wind, brushing against my skin and making me shiver. Was she laughing at me? Was this all just a game to her?

I reached my front door, my bare feet aching from the cold, hard ground. Mommy and Daddy were frantic, having found my empty bed. They embraced me, asking a million questions, but all I could do was cry and shake. I didn't bother telling them anything anymore.

The next few days were a blur of worried looks, whispered conversations, and visits to the doctor. They said I was sleepwalking, but I knew better. This was Elizabeth's doing. She had control over me, and she was getting stronger.

I stopped sleeping in my room, insisting on staying with my parents. They indulged me from time to time, but I could tell their patience was wearing thin. More often I ended up on the couch. They didn't believe in Elizabeth, and they thought I was just going through a phase. But Mommy knew. She must have known because she saw things too.

The school became a sanctuary, a place where Elizabeth couldn't reach me. But even there, I wasn't safe from her influence. My grades began to slip, my friendships withered, and I became a shadow of my former self. Jamie tried to help, but he was as lost as I was. He believed me, but he didn't know how to fight a ghost. We researched together, looking for ways to banish Elizabeth, but everything we tried failed.

Elizabeth was relentless. Her attacks grew more vicious, her presence more oppressive. I felt trapped, suffocated by her malice, unable to escape her grasp.

I reached my breaking point one night when I woke to find Elizabeth standing over my bed. Her eyes were black voids, her face twisted into a malevolent grin. She reached out to touch me, and I felt a searing pain, like fire, burning into my soul. I screamed and scrambled away, but she followed me, floating through the air, her voice a sibilant whisper in my ear.

Why are you afraid, Evie? I just want to play. Play with me, Evie. Forever and ever.

I ran from the room, sobbing, and found Jamie. He held me as I shook, unable to speak, unable to think. It was too much. I couldn't handle it anymore. I was losing myself to the fear, to the darkness that Elizabeth had brought into my life.

And that's when Jamie had an idea. It was dangerous, maybe even crazy, but it was our only hope. We would have to confront Elizabeth, to face her on her terms, and force her to leave us alone.

Together, we began to plan, knowing that our lives, our sanity, and our family's future depended on our success. We had to be strong, we had to be brave, and we had to be ready for the fight of our lives.

But deep down, I knew that Elizabeth was waiting for us. She wanted us to challenge her. She wanted to play her game.

And she wasn't going to play fair.

Chapter Nine—Mary

I could feel it in the air, a thick and suffocating tension, the kind that precedes a thunderstorm. The sky was clear, but the atmosphere was clouded with fear and suspicion, and I sensed that something terrible was on the horizon.

It was a Sunday, and Andrew and I were in our humble home, engaged in our domestic routines. My hands were busy with needlework, but my mind was elsewhere, filled with dread. The whispers had grown louder, the accusations more pointed, and the eyes of our neighbors were watching us with a newfound scrutiny.

A sudden commotion outside broke me from my troubled thoughts. Andrew rushed to the window, peering out with a furrowed brow. "Andrew, what dost thou see?" I queried, my voice trembling.

"They approach, Mary. A crowd," he replied, his eyes wide with terror. As we peered out, a mob, with the Kelly family at its head, was advancing upon our dwelling, their countenances filled with wrath. The door resounded with a harsh knocking, and Mr. Kelly's voice rang out. "Open this door, in the name of our Lord! Stand thee accused, Andrew and Mary Sanford!"

"We must confront them," said Andrew, though fear was in his eyes. "The Lord knoweth we are innocent." With a heavy heart, he opened the door, and we were faced with our accusers.

"Mary Sanford!" Mrs. Kelly declared, her eyes ablaze. "Thou hast been seen in consort with Goody Ayres, plotting the demise of our Elizabeth!" The crowd murmured their agreement, their faces set in judgment.

"No! 'Tis falsehood!" I exclaimed. "I held Elizabeth dear! I did nothing, Kit Kelly. Nothing at all!"

"Lies and deceit!" Mr. Kelly bellowed. "The proof is plain. Thou hast consorted with witches, and thine hands are tainted with innocent blood! Look! Look upon the body of my child, thou witch!"

I recoiled at the sight of the limp child in her father's arms. Andrew's face was pale, his eyes filled with shock. "I did no crime. I hurt not the child nor anyone!"

"We are upright and God-fearing," Andrew uttered, his voice faltering. "We have walked in the path of righteousness all the days of our lives. We would not bring harm to a child."

"The Lord's eye is all-seeing," Mrs. Kelly snapped, her eyes like slits. "And He shall judge thee for thy wickedness. My daughter is dead! My Elizabeth is dead!"

The crowd's voices rose in a fearful chorus, their accusations a crushing weight. I knew then that we were ensnared in a frenzy of mass hysteria, caught in a maelstrom of suspicion and fear.

The world had turned its back on us, and the storm was about to break. The crowd erupted into shouts and cries, their voices a cacophony of fear and hatred. I felt trapped, suffocated by their accusations, and I knew that our lives had been irrevocably altered.

And somewhere in the distance, the crows began to laugh and caw.

The dark clouds were gathering. As the crowd's fury swelled, a dark realization settled upon me. This was not merely a wave of anger; it was a tide that could drown us. We had to act, or we would be swept away.

"Stay thy hands, good people!" I implored, my voice rising above the cacophony. "Let us bring the body of dear Elizabeth within that we might see the truth!"

A hushed murmur spread through the crowd. They exchanged glances, and slowly, the intensity of their rage began to ebb. With cautious hands, Andrew and I allowed them to carry the lifeless form of Elizabeth inside. Her face was pale, her eyes closed, as though in peaceful slumber. But peace was far from this place. She was most certainly a dead child.

The crowd pressed in, their eyes wide, filled with a mixture of curiosity and suspicion. "Explain yourself, Mary Sanford. My daughter accused you before she left this world. Confess your crimes!"

I did my best to remain calm, although inside I was screaming. "I gave Goody Ayres naught but chickweed and anise to aid Elizabeth's ailments, as she bade me," I explained, my voice trembling with emotion. "She diagnosed the child with a bronchial ailment. I meant no harm to the little girl and only did as I was sought."

"But my child is dead, and she passed in great agony! It was poison thou delivered!" Mrs. Kelly cried; her voice filled with a mother's anguish. "Thou didst consort with that wicked witch! With whom else didst thou consort, Mary Sanford?"

"I tell thee true," I insisted, my eyes fixed on Mrs. Kelly's, "there is no malevolent deed to be found. You know my heart; I would never partake in such wickedness. Besides, I too am to be a mother. How can one mother do such evil to another?" My surprising news silenced them quickly. The room was thick with tension, the air heavy with mistrust. Then, a voice of reason rose above the fray.

"Enough!" Judge Marshall commanded, his eyes stern but not unkind. "The matter shall be decided in a court of law, under the watchful eyes of God. Until then, let us not pass judgment without due evidence. You cannot hang a woman ripe with child. Calm thyselves!"

Reluctantly, the crowd began to disperse, their eyes still filled with doubt and suspicion. The Kellys lingered a moment longer, their faces etched with grief and anger.

"Let the body of Elizabeth remain at River Run while the examiner comes to view her," Mrs. Kelly said, her voice choked with emotion. "Let her body testify against her killers."

I felt a chill run down my spine at her words, and as they departed, I knew that a shadow had fallen upon our lives. How could they leave their child's body here?

In the week that followed, the examiner did come, and of course he told us nothing. Elizabeth's body, which now smelled of death, was promptly buried, and we were forbidden to attend her funeral. We were shunned by our neighbors; cast out from the society we had once embraced. Friends turned away, eyes averted, and whispers followed us wherever we went.

The trial loomed like a dark cloud on the horizon, a storm that threatened to engulf us. And all the while, the haunting presence of Elizabeth's body at River Run served as a grim reminder of the terrible accusation that had been thrust upon us.

The world had turned against us, and we were alone. The days that followed were filled with a silence more profound than the mere absence of sound. It hung heavy in the rooms of River Run, a palpable weight that neither Andrew nor I could lift. From time to time, I heard a child crying. Whether it was my own or the late Elizabeth, I could not say, and I did not reveal this to Andrew.

I could see the torment in Andrew's eyes, the way they flickered with doubt and uncertainty when he looked at me. Was it fear, I wondered? Did he, too, question my innocence?

"Andrew, dost thou believe me?" I asked one cold evening as we sat by the hearth, the fire's glow casting long shadows on the walls.

He looked at me, his eyes wide with something I couldn't quite fathom. "Believe thee? How canst thou ask such a thing, Mary? I love thee, but this...this is tearing at my very soul."

I felt a sharp pang in my heart at his words, a wound that went deeper than any physical pain.

"I know," I whispered, tears welling in my eyes. "It tears at me, too. But we must trust in each other, Andrew. We must, for the sake of one another and our child."

He reached for my hand, his grip trembling, but firm. "I do trust thee, Mary. But the world has gone mad, and I fear what this madness may do to us."

We sat in silence, the fire crackling, the only sound in the room. I could feel the distance between us, a chasm that had opened, threatening to swallow us whole.

Days turned into nights, and the strain continued to grow. We moved through our daily chores like specters, our interactions hollow and devoid of the warmth that had once defined our relationship.

The trial was drawing near, and with it came a fear that was almost paralyzing. The world had turned its back on us, and we were left to face this terror alone. But more than the fear of the trial, more than the scorn of our neighbors, it was the growing rift between Andrew and me that weighed most heavily on my soul.

We were being tested, not just by the world but by each other. And as the days wore on, I couldn't shake the nagging fear that our love, once so strong and unbreakable, might not survive this ordeal.

The morning dawned cold and bleak, a fitting herald to the dread that filled my soul. Andrew had left for the neighboring town, a desperate quest for a new ox to keep our farm alive. His parting kiss was distant, his eyes filled with worry, not just for the trial but for what lay between us. He did not ask me to go, nor did I volunteer.

I busied myself with chores, the mundane tasks a thin veneer on the terror that gnawed at me. The whispers had grown louder, the accusations more brazen. And with each passing hour, a dark cloud seemed to loom closer.

Then they came.

A sharp knock echoed through the still house, and I felt a chill run down my spine. I knew, even before I opened the door, what awaited me.

Judge Marshall, flanked by two stern-faced men, stood at my threshold, his eyes hard and unyielding. "Mary Sanford, thou art accused of witchcraft. Thou must come with us to the court," he intoned, his voice devoid of warmth.

I felt the room spin, my legs threatening to buckle beneath me. But more than fear, it was a sudden, sharp pain in my belly that stole my breath. I clutched at my stomach, panic rising like bile in my throat. "I feel unwell, sir," I stammered, tears spilling from my eyes. "I fear I may miscarry."

Judge Marshall's eyes softened ever so slightly, but his voice remained firm. "We shall have the physician examine thee, but thou must come. It is the law."

They led me away, my home disappearing behind me, the pain in my belly a constant reminder of the life growing within me. A life now threatened by the madness that had gripped our town. But no doctor examined me. I was instead taken to the courthouse, which was full and running over with the curious. The court was full of hostile faces, the air thick with tension and accusation. My accusers gathered, their eyes gleaming with fury. The Kelly family, neighbors I had once considered friends, were now baying for my blood.

I was placed on the dock, my hands trembling, my heart pounding. All the while, the cramps continued, now a dull ache that filled me with terror.

I looked around the courtroom, my eyes seeking a friendly face, someone who might still believe in my innocence. But all I saw were friends that had somehow become strangers, their eyes filled with judgment and hate. I was alone, and the realization was like a knife to my heart. The trial was beginning, and where was Andrew? Had he known this would happen? *Is this why he left for the ox?*

I knew with a certainty that chilled me to the core that my life, and the life of my unborn child, hung in the balance.

I experienced a strange sort of detachment during the court proceedings. With the formalities of the accusation complete, they led me away in shackles to a small jail, a place more fit for animals than for humans. The cold, dank air filled my nostrils, each breath a sharp reminder of my fall from grace. The walls were damp and moss-covered, the floor a mix of mud and straw. I was cast into this pit, forsaken and forgotten.

In the dim corner of the cell lay Goody Ayres, her body frail and twisted. Madness danced in her eyes, a sickly glint that sent a chill down my spine.

Once, she had been a neighbor, even a friend. Now, she was a specter of herself, consumed by sickness and insanity. She did not speak to me but rather turned her back to me. She was covered in her own waste, and the smell sickened me.

They gave us water but no food. My pleas for sustenance were met with silence, my cries for my husband answered with scornful laughter. "Thou art a witch," they spat, "and witches need no food."

The days dragged on, each one a torment of hunger and despair. The pains in my abdomen came and went. I clung to the hope that Andrew would come, that he would find a way to save me. But as the days turned into weeks, that hope began to wither, a dying ember in the darkness. Occasionally, we were given bread to eat and sometimes a potato.

Goody's condition worsened, her mind unraveling with each passing hour. She began to hallucinate, her eyes wide and unseeing, her voice a hoarse whisper. At least she was speaking to me now, but what she said was madness.

"I see the devil," she would mutter, her fingers clawing at the air. "He comes for me, Mary. He comes!"

I tried to comfort her, but my words fell on deaf ears. Her mind was gone, lost to a world of terror and delusion. And then, one terrible night, she turned on me, her eyes wild, her voice filled with accusation.

"This be your fault!" she shrieked, her voice echoing through the jail. "It is you that is the witch, Mary Sanford! You have brought him here! You have damned us both!"

Her words were like a blade, cutting through me, her madness infecting my very soul. I denied it, trying to reason with her, but my denial was in vain. Her eyes bore into me, her words a relentless assault. The jailer came, his face twisted in disgust.

"Silence, witch!" He dragged Goody away, her screams fading into the distance. I was left alone, the silence deafening, her accusations ringing in my ears. As the days turned into an endless nightmare, I began to doubt myself, to question everything I knew.

I had never done anything so evil. I would never befriend the devil. The walls seemed to close in, as though the darkness longed to consume me. And through it all, Goody's words haunted me, a relentless echo of madness and despair.

"It is you that is the witch, Mary Sanford!"

Her voice became my reality, her madness my truth. And as I waited for a final trial that seemed as distant as the sun, I knew that I was lost, swallowed by a darkness from which there was no escape.

In that dismal jail, time became a cruel tormentor, each tick of the unseen clock a stabbing reminder of my abandonment. My body ached from hunger and thirst, my skin was caked with grime, and my soul was heavy with despair. My heart yearned for Andrew, for his strong arms to enfold me, for his reassuring voice to tell me all would be well. But he did not come, and I was left alone, forsaken by my husband and my community.

I tried to cling to faith, to believe in God's mercy, but doubt gnawed at me, my mind filled with dark thoughts and whispers of betrayal. I felt defeated, crushed by a weight I could not bear.

Then, without warning, it came—a sharp, agonizing pain that tore through me like a blade. I gasped, my hands flying to my stomach, my mind reeling. A sudden spurt of blood poured forth, staining my ragged clothes, a vivid reminder of my cruel reality.

The pain was unbearable, a searing, relentless agony that consumed me. I knew what it was, what it meant. My baby, my precious, unborn child, was being torn from me. I screamed—it was a primal, guttural cry that echoed through the jail, my body writhing, my mind filled with terror. The pain was unrelenting, each wave a fresh assault, each moment an eternity of suffering.

I begged for mercy, for release, for an end to the torment. I screamed for help, but there was no one to hear, no one to help. I was alone, utterly, and completely, lost in a world of pain and despair.

The miscarriage was a cruel twist of fate, a final, crushing blow. I felt my baby slip away, felt my hopes and dreams crumble into dust. My body was a battlefield, my soul a wasteland, my life a broken, shattered thing. As the hours dragged on, the pain subsided, leaving me empty and hollow. I lay on the cold, hard floor, tears mingling with blood, my body a twisted ruin, my spirit crushed.

My baby was gone; the tiny thing lay in my skirts. My husband was absent, my community turned against me. I was a pariah, an outcast, a woman bereft of all that she held dear.

In that dark, desolate place, I knew I had lost everything. There was nothing left but sorrow and despair, a never-ending night with no dawn in sight.

And through it all, Goody's words haunted me, a bitter refrain in my heart:

It is you that is the witch, Mary Sanford.

And perhaps, in my darkest moments, I began to believe it.

Chapter Ten—Sophia

The mystery of River Run had grown into an obsession with both Mike and me. We knew we were buying an old home, but this was beyond anything we could have imagined. A gnawing curiosity grew about what was happening here, and it was one that I could not ignore. The whispers of the past haunted me, ancient secrets hid in the shadows, waiting to be unearthed. More than anything, I wanted to protect Evie, who appeared to be the target of the malevolent presence.

With a newfound determination to get to the bottom of the activity, I enlisted the help of my family, and we embarked on a journey into the history of River Run, delving deep into the annals of time.

Of course, of the three children, only Jamie could help sort through books and papers, but he was good at it. He quickly scanned texts, looking for relevant keywords about witches and witchcraft. Mike didn't seem too crazy about the kids being involved, but why hide what we were doing? Almost everyone had had a paranormal incident.

After we finished tearing apart the home library, we took the kids to the library on the weekends. Noah and Evie buried their noses in Ramona and Dr. Seuss books while the rest of us scoured the dusty library and the creaking archive. Mike and I sifted through yellowed pages and weathered tomes while Jamie got interested in something else.

The documents we found "spoke" in hushed tones; their inked words a testament to forgotten lives and long-buried truths. People wanted to forget. I will never forget the librarian's face when I told her what we were looking for. She pointed us in the right direction but took no interest in helping us.

I didn't need a doctorate in history to tell me that the mid-1600s in Connecticut were a time of superstition and fear, a crucible of faith and fanaticism, where the unseen forces of the world were ever-present and often feared.

Yes, it was a different world back then. A very different world indeed.

The Salem witch trials were well known, but the Connecticut trials were shrouded in obscurity, a hidden chapter in the darker annals of Puritan New England. It was there, amid the grim testimonies and solemn judgments, that we stumbled upon the story of Mary and Andrew Sanford. The trial transcripts were missing, and when I asked about them, the librarian informed me that they'd been missing for hundreds of years. But she did give me a single sheet of paper, a copy of the results of the thirty-odd trials.

Two entries shocked me.

Andrew Sanford 1662 Acquitted

Mary Sanford 1662 Hanged

Mary's tale was a tragic one, marked by suspicion and betrayal, a grim reminder of humanity's capacity for cruelty. Accused of witchcraft along with Goody Ayres, Mary found herself trapped in a relentless web of fear and paranoia, her life unraveling in the cold embrace of Puritan justice.

As we delved deeper into the historical records, the terror of those times began to come alive. The accounts of the villagers were harrowing, filled with ominous details that sent shivers down my spine. The descriptions from the doomed child, Elizabeth Kelly, were some of the most frightening I'd ever heard, recounted with a fervor that suggested they were more than mere fabrications.

Clearly, the sick little one believed she saw something. Either that or she was fed a load of bull. That was Mike's thought.

"Weird they have no transcript of the trial but they have all the accusations detailed. Each and every one." Mike slid the book on the table and reached for another one. "Sophia, what are we doing, honey? Is this going to help? Will knowing help you? Or me? Or Evie? What about Noah?"

"Will not knowing help them?" I asked a bit too sarcastically. I didn't mean to sound that way, but it sure came out easily enough. "Sorry, Mike. Listen to this." I read a passage that shook me to the core. And there was more where that came from.

Descriptions of spectral visions and malevolent spirits, incantations, and mysterious potions were not merely fanciful tales but tangible realities that had shaped the lives of those involved. We were not the first residents of River Run to see the dead, to feel their rage. Each new detail seemed to claw at my soul, pulling me further into a nightmare from which I couldn't awaken.

The legal documents were a labyrinth of puritanical language, a reflection of a society governed by rigid morality and unyielding faith. Mike and I often laughed at our own understanding of the written testimony, but our laughter was hollow, forced, an attempt to shield ourselves from the horror that lay behind those words.

The overall reports conveyed the suffocating air of suspicion that settled like a pall over the community. Trust had been replaced with terror, love with loathing. The faces of friends and family had twisted into those of potential enemies, their glances filled with accusation and dread.

It was madness that had consumed the town, a hysteria born of ignorance and fear, and it had claimed Mary as its victim. Her innocence had been her downfall, her natural wisdom mistaken for malevolent magic.

How the hell did she get convicted and hanged, yet her husband got off completely?

Suddenly I could feel her, Mary Sanford. I could feel what she felt, could almost hear the cries of the accused, feel the chill of the prison cell, taste the bitterness of betrayal. River Run seemed to resonate with the echoes of that dark time, its very walls imbued with the pain and suffering of those who had once called it home.

The more we uncovered, the more I felt a creeping dread. The past was not content to lie dormant; it was reaching out, extending icy fingers that threatened to pull us into its dark embrace.

The Sanfords had been a prominent family, well-respected and influential, but they found themselves swept away by a wave of mass hysteria. It didn't matter that they were what might be considered high society. Friends turned into foes, neighbors into accusers, the bonds of trust and fellowship severed by the unforgiving blade of fear.

Elizabeth Kelly's death was the catalyst, a spark that ignited a wildfire of accusations and recriminations. The community was a tinderbox, and Mary Sanford's association with herbs and natural remedies made her an easy target. Her miscarriage, a private agony, became a public spectacle, a damning piece of evidence in the twisted logic of the witch-hunters. I couldn't believe what I was reading. Neither could Mike.

My eyes flickered with sadness as I read the details about Elizabeth Kelly's death, my voice trembling with emotion as I read it aloud. "The death of Elizabeth was more than just a loss; it was a spark that ignited a wildfire of fear and suspicion. You must understand, the community was a tinderbox back then, filled with terror of the unknown, superstition, and the harsh realities of Puritanical life. A single incident could lead to catastrophe."

Mike leaned back in his chair; his eyes clouded with the weight of history. "Mary Sanford, bless her soul, was different from others. She was known to use herbs and natural remedies to heal, something that was considered ungodly by many. When Elizabeth died, people were quick to turn their accusing fingers at her. Mary became an easy target, but like you, I can't believe her husband left her to face death alone."

I interjected, my voice broken and thoughtful, "It wasn't just the herbs that condemned her. In the twisted logic of the witch-hunters, it was seen as a sign of her guilt. And yeah, I agree with you. I couldn't imagine doing that to you—or you to me."

Mike nodded gravely. "Yes, the miscarriage was the final nail in her proverbial coffin. The townspeople, driven by fear, were ruthless. 'She's lost her child; she must be a witch,' they cried. 'God has punished her for her wicked ways.' They used her pain, her loss, as a damning piece of evidence." His voice caught, and he looked away, tears glistening in his eyes. Until this moment, I had no idea how this affected him too. I squeezed his hand reassuringly.

"Can you imagine? A woman, grieving the loss of her unborn child, accused of witchcraft, her every move scrutinized, her every tear a mark of guilt." I shook my head at the thought. "No wonder she's hanging around. But why would Elizabeth Kelly be in our house? She didn't live there. I don't see any records of that at all."

Mike's face was stern, his eyes dark with anger. "I have no idea. To be honest with you, I think this is all we're going to get from these books and files. Mary Sanford's tragedy was a chilling testament to the power of fear."

I could feel the library's temperature drop as Mike spoke. His face said it all. This all seemed like something impossible. Something out of a movie.

"The past is never truly gone," I whispered, almost to myself. "The echoes remain, especially in places like this. Mary's spirit is still there at the house, and she's not alone. I am afraid she's not alone. All this time, Evie was telling the truth. She told me the truth, and I didn't believe her, Mike."

Mike reached out and touched my hand, his fingers cold. "You believe her now. So do I. Don't beat yourself up, Sophia. Let's figure out the next steps. What I want to know is how could they not have told us about the history of the house when we bought it? That's unbelievable." Mike's words hung in the air, a solemn reminder of the fragility of justice and the eternal struggle between fear and reason.

We headed home. The kids had stacks of books, I took a few home too. We ordered pizza and Mike got lost in a game while I poked around yet another dusty history book. He said something to me, but I was only half listening. I nodded as I continued to read. I was tempted to pour myself another glass of whiskey, but the look on Mike's face broke my heart. I wasn't out of control, not like I used to be. I rarely drank anymore. Only since moving here had I had a sip or two. But it could happen. And I couldn't do that again.

The more I read, the more I was drawn into Mary's world, a dark and forbidding place where reason gave way to madness and compassion was a rare and fleeting thing. I felt a connection to her, a sympathetic resonance that transcended the centuries. For some reason, Mary Sanford must believe that I could help her, but help her do what?

Realizing I needed guidance, I decided to consult with someone more versed in the intricacies of Connecticut's past. The formerly unhelpful librarian, Matilda Burns, came to mind, and when I called her the following day, her attitude had changed. Yes, she said, she was more than eager to share the sordid story of Fairfield's past.

Matilda was a staple in the community. She was an elderly woman with a mane of silver hair, and she was the town's unofficial historian. Her eyes, sharp and discerning, held stories of generations past. I asked Jamie's teacher about her. She said that if you had a question about Connecticut's history, Matilda was the one to ask. Of course, I didn't tell the teacher that the house might be haunted.

Matilda agreed to meet us at River Run, curious about our findings. But to our surprise, she wasn't alone. Accompanying her was a tall, wiry man with a grizzled beard and intense eyes. He had a lovely presence, I immediately sensed that he was kind, and he was a snappy dresser.

"Good evening. This is my friend, Lee Lane. He has a particular interest in the unexplainable and has assisted me in a number of peculiar matters."

I shook Lee's offered hand. "It's an honor to meet you, Lee. I'm Sophia, and this is my husband, Mike. Welcome to River Run, both of you."

Mike smiled beautifully. "The pleasure's ours. We've been researching the history of River Run and uncovered some unsettling stories. We heard you might be able to fill in the gaps. We've got lots of them."

The older man, with a balding head and shiny green eyes, laughed. It sounded pretty and musical. "Unsettling indeed. Matilda told me about the recent events here. The past has a way of lingering, especially when there are unresolved matters. I hope you don't mind that I invited myself."

"Lee is being modest. He's an expert in the field of the paranormal. And if what you've told me about River Run is true, his expertise might prove invaluable."

I eyed Lee suspiciously. "You believe in ghosts, Mr. Lane?"

"I believe in energies, Mrs. Boyson, and sometimes they leave imprints on the world. Ghosts, spirits, call them what you will, they're manifestations of something that once was."

Mike closed the door behind our gathering as we ushered everyone into the living room. "We've felt something here, but it's hard to explain. It's like echoes of the past are trying to reach out to us."

"That's not uncommon in places with a history like River Run's. The echoes you speak of may be more tangible than you think." Lee nodded as he spoke.

"That's why we're here. To help you unravel this mystery. What say we take a tour of the house, and you can share what you've found? Are the kids home? I would like to meet them."

"They are visiting their grandmother tonight. I thought it would be better to keep them out of the house while we talk about this. They've been through enough. We'd love to take you for a walk-through. The history of this place is becoming more real to us every day."

As we began to move through the house, the air was thick with anticipation. We shared the unspoken understanding that we were on the brink of uncovering something extraordinary.

Lee had an air of solemnity about him, each movement deliberate, as if constantly attuned to the unseen. He carried with him an assortment of tools—dowsing rods, pendulums, and EMF detectors. "Every old place has tales," he murmured, glancing around, "but not all wish to share them openly. This place feels ready to talk. I imagine it has been communicating in some way or another."

After the tour, we gathered in the living room again. Matilda spread out her research on the wooden coffee table, her eyes darting over the yellowed papers and aged photographs. "The Sanfords," she began, "were indeed significant in this town. But not all the history was written."

Lee nodded, his eyes distant. "Spirits hold on to places of significance. Pain, love, betrayal—emotions anchor them." He slowly walked around, holding out a pair of dowsing rods. As he approached a particular corner, the rods swayed, drawing closer together. "There's a presence here, a residual energy."

Matilda's voice was a soft whisper, "Mary Sanford's spirit, perhaps, seeking justice or maybe peace." She then recounted tales passed down in hushed voices through generations—tales of how Mary's spirit had been sighted wandering the fields, of strange occurrences in the vicinity, and of the cries that echoed on windless nights.

Lee, deeply engrossed in his equipment, suddenly paused. "She's here. And she wants to communicate."

Chills raced down my spine. The tales of River Run, Mary Sanford, and the witch trials had transformed from historical accounts to a palpable, eerie reality. We were no longer mere readers; we were becoming a part of the story itself.

I glanced around River Run, feeling its presence more acutely now. The shadows seemed to reach out, the floorboards groaned as if in agony, and I felt as though the very walls were whispering the secrets of the past.

"This place," I murmured, "it's alive with emotions."

Lee nodded, his eyes dark and knowing. "The echoes of the past are still here, Sophia, trapped within these walls."

The chapter of the Sanfords ended with unimaginable tragedy. Mary was convicted, her life torn away by the very people she had once called neighbors. Andrew's fate was lost to history, a blank page that seemed to mock our search for answers. But River Run stood firm, a silent and brooding witness.

As we finally gathered around a pot of coffee at the dining room table, Matilda unraveled the story of Mary and Andrew Sanford. How Mary was left to face the mob alone, lost her child, and was ultimately hanged. Andrew, it was rumored, ran away. Others say Mary didn't die at the gallows. Her dark lord empowered her to escape, and she walked out into the freezing snow and died. Nobody truly knew. Matilda confessed that she did not have a real opinion but that it was fascinating.

"If I were just listening to history, I would find it fascinating, but that's not the case. Evie has seen a girl she calls Elizabeth; we assume that's Elizabeth Kelly. I have seen Mary. These spirits aren't telling us why they're here. Elizabeth seems more evil, much more determined to cause harm."

The air grew cold, the candles Lee had lit stuttered and died, and we were plunged into an unnatural darkness.

A sound filled the room, a wail so mournful and full of agony that it seemed to come from the very depths of despair. It vibrated through me, resonating with something deep and primal.

"It's her," Lee's whisper broke through the terror, his face as white as a sheet. "Mary Sanford. She's here."

I felt it then, a presence that filled the room, a sensation of grief and longing so powerful it took my breath away. River Run seemed to tremble with the pain of a tormented soul.

And then, as quickly as it had come, it was gone.

We were left in stunned silence, the haunting cry still echoing in our ears. River Run had spoken, and its message was terrifyingly clear: the wounds of history were not healed, and the past was very much alive within these walls.

The ghost of Mary Sanford had reached out, and I knew then that we were inexorably linked to her story. Her pain, her longing, her injustice—they had become a part of us, a haunting melody that would remain with us forever.

"It's you, Sophia. She's attached herself to you. She wants to show you her life. How odd..." Lee chewed his bottom lip thoughtfully as he studied me.

"What do you mean attached to Sophia? Attached how?" That was Mike, worried as usual.

"I don't think it was Mary that attacked Mike. And I can't figure out why Elizabeth is scaring Evie so much. She was a child when she died. It's all so confusing." Lee sighed in frustration. "It must have been Elizabeth that attacked Mike. Mary doesn't have that kind of energy."

"Whoever or whatever it was, it was damn strong." Mike glanced at Matilda, who nodded knowingly.

"For now, I think we can reach out to Mary safely," Matilda said. "She's still here. Just on the edge of this realm. She's close because of you, Sophia. You share a bond somehow. She wants to show you something, something important."

"Me? Why me?" I asked as I sat on the couch nervously. I knew the answer, but I didn't want to believe it. Mary was fixated on me because she too had lost a child. Could that be it? "What do you have in mind? I don't think I'm down for a séance. It seems pointless if she's already here."

Lee nodded his head. "Agreed. Séances are summoning. We don't need to summon Mary Sanford. Mike, why don't you sit beside your wife? Matilda, come sit by me. Let's all relax and chat for a while, give Mary a chance to see that this is a safe environment."

I swallowed nervously. "Then what? Wait until she jumps on me?"

"No. Try to remain calm. Let's just wait and see what she says or does. Mary will return quickly."

He wasn't wrong.

Almost immediately, I heard Mary sighing in my ear...

Chapter Eleven—Mary

The courthouse was a humble yet oppressive structure, its wooden beams aged and worn, creaking under the weight of stern justice. It stood as a tangible embodiment of our community's rigid morality, a place where innocence and guilt were dissected under the unyielding scrutiny of Puritan law.

A hushed murmur filled the room as we were led in, hands bound, heads bowed. The air was thick with judgment, and I could feel the eyes of the crowd boring into us, their whispers a low and sinister hum. The very walls seemed to close in, as if conspiring to suffocate us. To my utter surprise, my husband was already in the dock as one of the accused.

I dared to steal a glance at Andrew, but his eyes were fixed ahead, face as pale as death. A pang of betrayal and confusion tore through me. Why would he not look at me? What had become of the love and trust we once shared?

Judge Marshall took his seat, his stern face reflecting the gravity of the occasion. The crowd fell into silence, their anticipation palpable.

"Bring forth the accused," the prosecutor announced, his voice cold and authoritative.

We were guided to the stand, the weight of our chains a cruel reminder of our predicament. The prosecutor's eyes met mine, filled with righteous condemnation.

"Mary Sanford, thou dost here stand accused of witchery, of trafficking with the Evil One, and of bringing about the demise of Elizabeth Kelly," he pronounced, his words resounding throughout the chamber. "And in thy wickedness, thou hast suffered thy child to miscarry in service to the foul adversary."

A collective gasp erupted from the crowd, followed by angry cries and hisses. The room seemed to spin, and I felt the world slipping away.

"Mary, how couldst thou?" Andrew's voice did cut through the tumult, a poniard to mine heart. His visage was contorted in torment, his eyes at last finding mine, brimming with treachery and incredulity. The room swayed, and a black fog clouded my vision. My legs gave way, and the floor rushed up to meet me.

The last thing I heard before succumbing to darkness was the ominous murmur of the crowd, a chilling prelude to the judgment that awaited us.

"Sirs, I have enacted no such deed, nor have I made a covenant with man, beast, or Lucifer. I am a stranger to any such agreement. Heretofore, I believed my wife, Mary Sanford, to be a virtuous and godly woman. A woman who did love the Lord. Now, with the loss of our offspring, I am lost in what to believe. Sirs, I stand innocent!"

The walls of the courtroom seemed to close in around me as the trial wore on, each testimonial a crushing blow to my very soul. I felt as if I were drowning in a sea of betrayal, gasping for breath as wave after wave of accusations crashed over me.

Andrew's face, once a source of comfort, was now a mask of cold indifference. He sat across from me, eyes averted, as if my very presence were a stain upon his honor. His silence was a wound that cut deeper than any words could. Had our love meant so little?

Had the loss of our child, a grief that weighed upon my heart like a millstone, become but a reason to condemn me?

One by one, our neighbors and friends took the stand, their voices tinged with fear and suspicion. Each word was a nail in my coffin, their memories of me twisted into grotesque caricatures by the dark cloud of witchcraft.

"Mary Sanford did conspire with Goody Ayres," one testified, his voice trembling. "I did see her gather herbs and chant incantations under the pale moon."

Another spoke, her voice high and shrill, "She looked upon my child with an evil eye, and he fell sick. 'Twas her wickedness that brought the malady."

I wanted to cry out, to protest their lies and plead my innocence. But my voice was trapped within me, a prisoner of my despair. The faces of the jury were impassive, their eyes unyielding, their minds made up.

The prosecutor's words were a cold and relentless hammer, chipping away at my sanity. "She hath forsaken God and embraced the devil's dark arts. Her very womb rejected the innocent child, a clear sign of her guilt."

I felt my strength ebbing away, the room a swirling vortex of accusation and condemnation.

The baby we had longed for, the child we had lost, was now a weapon against me. My heart ached with a pain beyond bearing, a grief so profound that I feared it would consume me.

The hours wore on, each one a torment, each a bleak and lonely abyss. I was lost, adrift in a world that had turned against me, a community that had once been my home now a hostile and unforgiving place. I clung to my faith, a fragile lifeline in a storm of madness. But even that seemed to slip through my fingers, a distant and elusive comfort.

In the end, all that remained was the hollow echo of my own despair, a haunting refrain that whispered of betrayal, loss, and a love that had died a slow and agonizing death.

The trial had broken me, but it was the abandonment, the cold and merciless judgment of those I had loved, that had truly destroyed me. It would not be the hangman's noose that killed me but my husband's abandonment.

The courtroom was filled with the murmur of voices, the whispering of gossip and fear. The prosecutor, a stern man with piercing eyes, called my husband to the stand. My heart ached as Andrew rose, his face pale, his shoulders slumped. There was a hollow emptiness in his eyes, a void where once there had been warmth and love.

"So, Goodman Sanford," the prosecutor began, his voice cold and unfeeling, "Thou art the husband of the accused, art thou not?"

"Aye, sir, I am," Andrew replied, his voice barely above a whisper.

"And canst thou vouch for thy wife's whereabouts and actions at all times? Canst thou say with certainty that she hath not consorted with witches or engaged in wicked practices?"

Andrew's eyes met mine, and in that moment, I saw a flicker of doubt, a shadow of uncertainty. My heart sank, a cold dread settling in the pit of my stomach.

"No, sir, I cannot," he said, his voice breaking. "I was oft away from home, tending to our lands and beasts. I know not what she did in mine absence."

A gasp went up from the crowd, a collective intake of breath that seemed to suck the very air from the room. I felt a sharp stab of betrayal, a pain so intense that I nearly cried out.

"Andrew," I heard myself whisper in despair.

"So, thou wert not around all the time?" the prosecutor pressed, his eyes narrowing.

"No, sir, I was not," Andrew replied, his voice faltering.

"Andrew?" I asked again.

His words were a dagger to my heart; this was a betrayal that cut deeper than any physical wound. My own husband, the man I had loved and trusted, had turned against me. I felt the walls closing in, the room spinning, my vision blurring.

"Mary, how couldst thou?" Andrew's voice reached my ears, a distant cry of anguish and confusion. I looked at him, tears welling in my eyes, but I could find no words to answer him.

I screamed in agony. My heart felt as if a dozen knives stabbed at it. I heard voices, distant and muffled, but they made no sense. Darkness closed in, and I felt myself falling, falling into a bottomless abyss of despair.

I awoke to a sharp slap upon my face, my eyes fluttering open to see the stern visage of the prosecutor peering down at me. Around me, the courtroom was a cacophony of whispers, stares, and accusing glares. My mind was a whirl, my body numb.

"Stand up, woman!" the prosecutor barked. "The court will not suffer thy theatrics."

I stumbled to my feet, my legs weak, my heart pounding. My eyes sought Andrew, but he had turned away, his face hidden in his hands. He was weeping like a child. The pain of his betrayal was a wound that would not heal, a betrayal that would fester and consume me. How dare he weep before me?

But the worst was yet to come. The testimony of Goody Ayres was the most damning of all. Her eyes wild and unfocused, her body wracked by illness and madness, she screamed at me, her voice filled with rage.

"It is thee, Mary Sanford! Thee and thy wicked potions! Thee who consorted with the Devil and brought this curse upon us all! This evil was done by thy order! You killed the good child! You made Elizabeth Kelly suffer!"

I shook my head, tears streaming down my face. "I am no witch," I whispered, my voice barely audible. "I have done no wrong."

But my protests fell on deaf ears, my pleas for mercy lost in a tide of hatred and fear. The evidence was circumstantial, the accusations baseless, but it mattered not. The die was cast, and my fate was sealed.

As the sun dipped below the horizon, casting a blood-red glow over the land, the gavel fell, the sentence passed.

Guilty. The word echoed in my mind, a death knell that signaled the end of all I had known and loved. My eyes met Andrew's one last time, but there was no forgiveness, no understanding in his gaze. Only accusation, only betrayal. He had abandoned me, left me to face the storm alone.

As the magistrate's rough hands pulled me away, I knew that my life, as I had known it, was over. The world had turned against me, and I was lost, adrift in a sea of despair and terror.

With the verdict, a murmur spread through the court like wildfire as my beloved Andrew, the one I had thought my truest ally, had turned his back on our sacred vows.

The magistrate turned a scrutinizing gaze toward Andrew. "Having examined thy conduct and testimony, and finding no evidence against thee, thou art hereby cleared of any association with witchcraft," he pronounced.

I watched in abject horror as Andrew nodded, a grim expression painted across his face.

"Thank ye, sir," he muttered, a mere whisper but one laden with the weight of decisions made.

With not a single glance in my direction, he made haste, exiting the courthouse. The wooden door closed behind him, and the finality of that sound struck deep, marking the chasm that had grown between us. I stared at the door, half daring to believe that it would open and that he would return. I hoped against hope to hear his voice call out in my defense.

But all I met was the cruel silence of abandonment.

My hands trembled, restrained by coarse ropes, as they tightened, drawing blood. Every face in the room seemed a blur of judgment and disdain, save for a few that held pity's soft glint. However, pity was a double-edged sword; it did little to comfort me in the face of overwhelming desolation.

The evening's chill began to creep into the building, the feeble candles flickering in the drafty room, casting eerie, dancing shadows upon the walls of the simple courthouse. The dim light seemed to mirror my waning hope, casting everything into a grim, foreboding darkness.

"Do you have any words in your defense?" the magistrate's voice boomed, breaking my stupor. But words had forsaken me.

My voice, once strong and unwavering, was reduced to a choked whisper. "I am innocent...I beg of thee, see reason." But the magistrate's steely gaze offered no solace.

"The court will reconvene on the morrow to decide thy fate, Mary Sanford."

As the court disbanded, I was dragged away, the cold stones of the jail cell awaiting me.

Left to the mercy of a vengeful community, with naught but the cold walls, filtered moonlight, and my thoughts for company, despair threatened to consume me whole. The night was a cacophony of distant sounds, muffled cries, and cold whispers, all blending into a surreal symphony that echoed through the dark recesses of my cell. Sleep eluded me, as did hope. The coldness of the stone beneath me was a bitter reminder of my reality—a world that had turned against me, a love that had forsaken me.

Days turned into nights, each indistinguishable from the other, a blur of waiting, longing, and soul-crushing fear. The only reprieve came from brief visits by Sarah Miles.

The stillness of the night was interrupted only by the distant murmurs from the townspeople outside, their whispers akin to the rustling of dried leaves. I suddenly thought of the crows, the many crows that announced my doom. Where were they now? Had the crows fled with Andrew?

"Mary...Mary Sanford," a hushed voice called out from the adjacent cell. I turned my head to find the weary eyes of Goody Ayres staring back at me. Her condition had worsened since our last encounter. The pallor of her skin contrasted starkly with the fiery madness in her gaze.

"Dost thou believe me now? Dost thou see the devilry that hath befallen us?" she rasped.

"Goody Ayres," I did whisper back, my throat as dry as the barren earth, "I never wished for any of this foulness. Our aims were pure and righteous. Thou knowest that truth. Why wouldst thou utter falsehood and say otherwise? Thou hast doomed us, Goody!"

She let out a mirthless laugh. "Intentions weigh naught in the eyes of those who perceive but shadows and specters."

A chill ran down my spine. For in her madness, Goody Ayres held a kernel of truth. The shadow of fear and superstition had blinded our community to reason, casting both of us into the heart of this storm.

The following morning, the sound of hurried footsteps approached my cell. A silhouette stood before the bars, cloaked in shadows. "Mary," a familiar voice whispered. To my shock, it was Sarah again, a dear friend I had known since childhood.

"Sarah! Oh, God's grace, what brings thee back here? I told thee last time not to return."

She pressed a small bundle through the bars, her eyes darting around nervously. "None of that, Mary. Eat. You need your strength," she implored. Inside the bundle were morsels of bread and cheese. Though humble, it was a feast for my starved body.

"Sarah, why? After all the town says..."

She shushed me, her voice tremulous, "I know you, Mary. The heart knows truth, even when the world is blinded by lies."

A tear rolled down my cheek. In this abyss of despair, Sarah's act was a beacon, a glimmer of humanity. "Bless you," I murmured.

Sarah glanced around one last time and whispered, "Hold on, Mary. Not all have forsaken thee."

"Andrew? He hast seen reason? He will rescue me?"

Sarah shook her head and glanced around to make sure no one saw or heard her. "Not Andrew, but another is coming. He shall help you, Mary. Do not refuse him."

Before I could ask any further questions, Sarah fled. As her footsteps faded, I was once more alone with my thoughts. Though the path was dark and uncertain, the spark of hope, ever so faint, had reignited within me.

Maybe somehow God would see me through.

Chapter Twelve—Sophia

The sunlight was beginning to dip below the horizon, casting an orange glow over the yard as I looked out the kitchen window. Dinner was simmering on the stove, and the children were scattered throughout the house, each absorbed in their own activities.

Jamie was in the basement, engrossed in a new video game, Evie was reading in her room, and little Noah was playing with his toys in the living room. I took a deep breath, trying to shake off the ominous feelings that had been plaguing me since we started digging into the history of River Run.

I was about to call everyone for dinner when a piercing scream erupted from the basement. I dropped the spoon I was holding and ran, my heart pounding in my ears.

"Jamie!" I shouted, my voice trembling as I reached the basement door.

I threw it open and found Jamie, his face pale and eyes wide, staring at something in the corner of the room.

"M-Mom," he stammered, pointing, "she was here. An old lady! She had on an apron and a hat. You know, like a pilgrim! She was evil! Her face was twisted, and her eyes were black!"

I followed his gaze but saw nothing, only the shadows playing on the walls. A chill ran down my spine, and I hurriedly grabbed Jamie's hand, pulling him upstairs.

"It's okay, honey. I believe you. You're safe now," I whispered, but I couldn't shake the fear that had settled in my chest. "She's gone." Was she gone? I couldn't be sure. I gave Jamie a glass of water and then gathered all the children into the living room with me. We would wait here until Mike got home from work. That was the only plan I had. I turned on the television and decided to serve dinner in the living room as Mike was clearly running late.

To my great relief, nothing else happened. But when Mike came home, he didn't have to ask. He could see the fear on our faces.

That night, Noah woke screaming, his small body wracked with terror, his eyes wide with something I couldn't fathom. He would point to the corner of his room, crying about the "bad man" who wanted to hurt him.

The demon's torments—that's what I secretly called it—grew more pronounced, more malevolent. Objects would move on their own, doors would slam shut, and Noah would be found, crying, in places he couldn't have reached alone. The evil had moved on from Evie, who was now a shell of herself, to Noah.

Mike and I were literally at our wit's end with all this. We began searching the newspapers for cheap rentals but with no luck. There were even talks of layoffs at his company.

As the days turned into weeks, the hauntings grew more intense, the boundaries between the earthly and the supernatural blurring. We were caught in a web spun centuries ago, and I knew that if we didn't find a way to break free, we might never escape.

River Run seemed to breathe with a life of its own, a dark and twisted soul that held us in its grip. It was alive with the echoes of the past, and I feared what it might do next.

The terror was no longer confined to the shadows; it was real, tangible, and closing in. Our family was unraveling, and I knew that we had to act. Time was running out, and the haunting was far from over.

Night after night, we were haunted. The relentless ghosts gave no reprieve. One evening, as we were settling into the uneasy sleep that had become our norm, a chilling laugh echoed through the house. It was not a human laugh but something twisted and malevolent, followed by the soft, haunting melody of a lullaby that seemed to come from the very walls. Though we searched, the source eluded us, leaving us shaken and more frightened than ever.

As the days wore on, the paranormal activity escalated, each incident more terrifying and inexplicable than the last. Objects would move on their own, doors would slam shut, and disembodied whispers would fill the air, growing louder and more urgent as though demanding something we could not understand.

Then, the unthinkable happened.

I was in the kitchen one evening, the house quiet and the children presumably asleep, when I heard a soft, eerie giggle from upstairs. It was a sound both familiar and alien, a joyful childlike laugh twisted by something dark and unnatural.

"Evie?" I called, fear clawing at my throat.

I raced upstairs, my heart pounding, only to find her room empty, the window open, curtains dancing like ghostly apparitions in the wind. A cold dread settled in my stomach, and a voice inside me screamed that something terrible had happened.

"Evie!" I screamed, panic consuming me. "EVIE!"

I looked out the window, and my blood turned to ice. There she was, standing at the edge of the dark forest, her hand held by her stuffed rabbit toy, Stuffy. Its cold blue eyes were shining, gleaming with malevolence, and its head spun around, grinning at me with a wicked, knowing smile. It was walking beside her, guiding her, luring her into the shadows.

"Mommy," Evie whispered, her voice carried by the wind, her eyes wide with a terror that mirrored my own. Even from this distance, I recognized it. I was frozen, a cold horror gripping me. The ghosts had not just tormented us; they had taken her.

I could hear Mike behind me, his voice filled with concern, but there was something in his tone that sent a chill down my spine. Mike was suddenly right beside me.

"Sophia, wait! Let's think this through!"

I held onto his hand, needing his strength, his warmth, but what met my fingers was ice cold. I turned to look at him, and the scream died in my throat.

Mike's face had morphed, his eyes black and soulless, his mouth twisted into a cruel smile. This was not my husband! This was the demon that had been tormenting us.

"Sophia," it purred, its voice a mockery of Mike's gentle tone, "you can't save her. She's mine now. They are all mine. So are you!"

I stumbled back, horror washing over me as it reached for me, its fingers like claws. Pain exploded in my chest as it dug into me, its laugh a twisted symphony of malice and triumph.

And then, I woke up.

I was in my bed, the familiar smells of dinner rising from the lower floor. How had I gotten here? I was disoriented, my heart pounding, the terror still fresh in my mind.

"Everything okay, honey? Is supper ready?" Mike's voice, warm and loving, came from the hallway. I turned to see him, my real Mike, concern in his eyes. I rushed to him, tears streaming down my face, needing to feel his arms around me, to know that it was just a nightmare.

"Hey," Mike held me close. "It's okay, honey."

But as he held me, I couldn't shake the feeling that it was more than just a dream. The haunting was real, the terror was real, and something had changed. We were no longer just victims; we were part of it, woven into the very fabric of the nightmare that was River Run.

And the dark shadows that had been content to lurk in the corners were closing in, ready to make their move.

Our nightmare was far from over, and the real terror was just beginning.

Chapter Thirteen—Mary

The days had become a torturous blur, each one a heavy stone upon my heart. Locked in this wretched cell, the taste of despair was ever present, souring even the air I breathed. I was to be hanged; my soul condemned for a sin I did not commit. The only window to the world was a small slit in my cell, through which I had witnessed Goody Ayres' punishment. They whipped her, the cruel leather tearing her flesh, the sound of her cries cutting through me like a blade. I had wept for her, for me, for the cruel twist of fate that had brought us here.

How had any of this happened? We weren't witches—just two women that wished to help people. How had this fate befallen us? I prayed, oh, how I had prayed. I begged the Lord for a sign, for a flicker of hope in this suffocating darkness. But my pleas were met with silence, the emptiness echoing my own desolation.

Where was this rescuer that Sarah spoke of? They would hang me any day!

Night fell, and with it came a cold that seemed to seep into my very bones. I huddled in the corner of my cell, the chains that bound me clinking softly, a constant reminder of my impending doom.

"O Lord, why hast Thou forsaken me?" I whispered, my voice breaking. "What have I done to deserve this fate?" I waited, listened, but there was no response. Only the shadows seemed to answer, shifting and whispering in a language I could not comprehend.

The night wore on, and sleep was a distant dream, the fear and despair gnawing at me, keeping me awake. Then, as the clock in the jailer's office chimed midnight, I sensed something. A presence, a darkness that was more than just the absence of light. I looked up, and there he was.

A shadow man, his form distinct, his eyes two glowing embers in the blackness. Fear gripped me, but I could not look away.

"Mary," he said, his voice like silk, "I alone can save you."

I gasped, the words taking a moment to register. "Save me? How? Who are you?"

He stepped closer, his form becoming more defined, yet he altogether remained a shadow. "I am one who can offer you a chance, a way out of this doom. But it comes with a price. My price."

"A price?" My heart was pounding, hope and terror warring within me. "What price, sir? Why can I not see you?"

He smiled, a twisted, cruel thing. "A promise, a bond. You will owe me, lovely Mary, and when the time comes, you will pay me."

His words left me cold, even colder than I already was, but I could think of nothing to say. I stared at the shadowy thing, my mind reeling. This was madness. I had finally gone mad—like Goody Ayres! Was this shadow proposing that I make a deal with a devil? Was this the devil before me?

I could not think properly, but even in my madness, I knew that the gallows awaited me, the noose, a cold and unyielding judgment.

"I...will make no deal with you," I stammered, tears welling in my eyes. "I want to live, but not at your price! You want my soul!"

"The cost is for me to decide," he replied, his voice soft, almost tender. "Did I say I require your soul? The question is, do you want to live? Do you want to escape this fate, to have a chance at life again?" He squatted before me and by my soul, his face took on familiar features. Andrew! He looked like Andrew!

Oh, yes, I am quite mad!

"Not mad, Mary Sanford. You are not mad, lovely Mary."

Not my soul? He wouldn't take my soul?

"Don't look like him! Don't!" I closed my eyes and prayed that he would leave, but he did not. I knew this without looking because his presence brought with him an undeniable testimony. The hairs on my body were standing on end, my stomach flipped within me, and stranger still, I burned with great desire for this shadow.

Why do I feel like a wanton woman when I am faced with the devil?

"Open your eyes, Mary Sanford."

I could not resist. To my great relief, he looked no longer like my Andrew but again was merely a shadow. I looked into his eyes, those burning coals, and I knew that this was a path from which there was no return. It was a choice between certain death and an uncertain future, a gamble with my very soul. I should not believe him. I should not trust him. But I did not want to die. My desperation won, the need to live, to breathe, to feel the sun on my face again.

I nodded, tears streaming down my face. I whispered, "I do not wish to die. Not for this unfair crime."

The shadow man's smile widened, and I saw terribly sharp, white teeth. I should have screamed, said the Lord's Prayer, but he reached out, his hand cold and insubstantial, yet somehow solid, and I did not flinch. "Then it is done. You will live, lovely Mary. But remember, the debt must be paid—when the time comes."

"When the time comes." I repeated what he said, and my heart felt dark, dead and heavy. I had no idea what he meant, but I realized immediately that I had made a wrong deal.

I had done the wrong thing.

How disappointed my husband would be in me. But I was disappointed in him too, wasn't I? Andrew had abandoned me and had saved me not.

With those words, he stepped back and was gone, the darkness receding, leaving me alone in my cell, my heart pounding, my soul trembling. I had made a deal, a pact with a being I did not perceive. I had chosen life, but at what cost?

I began to laugh. I laughed long and hard, and it was the sound of madness. When I could laugh no more, emptiness settled in my empty soul. The night wore on, the hours ticking away, each one a step closer to my salvation, or perhaps my damnation. Only time would tell.

Three days passed, each one an eternity of waiting, the shadow man's words a constant whisper in my mind. The terror of the gallows had been replaced by a new fear, a fear of the unknown, of the dark bargain I had struck.

Then, on the third night, it happened.

The clock struck midnight, and a strange wind began to howl, a mournful wail that seemed to come from the very bowels of the earth. My cell door shuddered and groaned, and then, with a sound like a scream, it burst open.

I stumbled out, my body weak and trembling, my mind a whirl of confusion and dread. The jail was empty, the guards and prisoners alike seemingly blind to my presence.

The door slammed shut behind me, locking with a finality that sent a chill down my spine. I was free, but at what cost?

I laughed a mad sound. I expected at any moment to be recaptured, but no one came to retrieve me. Could they truly not see me? Was I dead? A spirit, perhaps, invisible to the naked eye?

I wandered the dark streets, the wind tugging at my clothes, the shadows whispering my name. I was a slave to the darkness now, bound by a pact that demanded payment.

But I did not walk alone. The shadow man walked with me, his voice a seductive promise, his eyes a pit of endless hunger.

Lovely Mary, you must offer souls to your dark lord. You must help satisfy my endless thirst. If not, I will require your soul—and the souls of all you love. Use your magic, Lovely Mary. Serve me!

I wept at his words, but what could I do? I did as he bade me and traveled where he led me. First, to the cemetery. It was a dark and forlorn place in the blackness of night.

My first task had been to claim Elizabeth Kelly; her soul would be a sacrifice to my new master. I could not explain how I knew the words, but I knelt at her grave and summoned her spirit up, up, up and into my hands.

Then there were others to capture, Goody Ayres being one. Others I knew, some I did not, each one a step further into darkness for me. Each capture was another dark mark upon my soul. I was lost, a puppet to forces I could not comprehend, my life a twisted maze of fear and despair.

My dark lord led me to a small cottage in the forest, a suitable place for a witch such as I. I woke daily to bread and wine and, at times, other things. I crept around the woods and gathered herbs and fruits, bones and blood, everything I needed to do my service and keep my life.

No one came for me. No one searched for Mary Sanford, but if they came, I was no longer afraid. I would not be treated as before. My master would never allow it.

Nightly I wandered the village unseen, watching through windows, leaving my mark on certain houses. And yet, there was one more soul I must claim, one more debt I must pay.

Andrew! You will not escape me! My betrayer!

I found myself standing before River Run again, the house looming in the darkness, its windows like dead eyes. I came back to find him, but he never returned.

But the devil must have his due. Even if I could not find Andrew, I knew what I must do, and yet my heart ached, my soul crying out in protest. I reached out, my mind touching this new one. Sophia was her name.

"Sophia," I whispered in her dream, my voice a mournful plea. "Forgive me. I need Evie's soul—and yours too."

She did not hear me at first, but night after night, I warned her. I promised her. Until one night, when I could feel the dark lord drawing close. If I did not take them this night, he would do the deed himself, and his taking would be much more painful. And also, I would be done forever.

It is better this way, Sophia. Give me Evie. Give yourself to me, and that will be enough!

Her scream was a dagger in my heart, her terror a reflection of my own. I had become a monster, a creature of darkness, my humanity lost to a bargain I could not escape. I fled into the night, the wind howling, the shadows reaching for me, my soul a barren wasteland.

I was damned, condemned to wander the earth, a slave to the darkness, my every step a reminder of the price I had paid.

When had I died? I could not say, but dead I was for sure. Dead, and soulless.

And in the depths of my despair, I knew that there was no escape, no redemption. The shadow man's laugh echoed in my ears, a haunting melody that promised only more suffering, more pain.

I was his, body and soul, forever.

And there was no way out. I could postpone it, but not for much longer. I was death's slave, and I would take the child, and then another, and then I would take them all.

I had no choice...

Chapter Fourteen—Sophia

I woke up screaming, my heart pounding in my chest, sweat soaking my skin. The nightmare had been so real, so vivid. Mary's face, her mournful eyes, her desperate plea—they were etched into my mind.

"Evie! Evie!" I yelled, jumping out of bed and rushing to her room. I needed to see her, to touch her, to know she was safe.

"Sophia? What's wrong?" Mike called, following me, genuine concern in his voice.

"It's Mary," I stammered in a whisper, tears in my eyes as I held Evie close, feeling her warm breath, the gentle rise and fall of her chest. "She wants her soul, Mike. And mine. She's coming for Evie. She's not good! Not at all!" As if she heard me, my little girl moaned in her sleep.

Mike's face went pale, and he reached out, taking my hand as I put her back and covered her up. "It was just a dream, Soph. Just a nightmare. Come on. Let Evie rest."

I shook my head, looking into his eyes, seeing my own fear reflected there. "No, it wasn't just anything. It was real! I could feel Mary, hear her. She's trapped, Mike. She's become something...something dark and evil. The devil came to her. She was a witch! Not at first, but he changed her! Oh God, Mike! I've been wrong about her."

"Sophia, calm down!" Mike's voice was urgent, his eyes wide as he tried to make sense of my words. "It was a nightmare, that's all. It's the stress of everything that's happened. You need rest. Come back to bed or you'll wake up the children. They've been through enough. We all have." Together we stumbled out into the hallway and kept our voices down.

I shook my head, tears streaming down my face, my heart still racing from the vivid terror of the dream. "No, Mike. It was real. I could feel her, hear her. She's desperate, trapped. I mean it when I say she's coming for Evie and me. I saw the whole scene. She showed me what happened. Mary was facing the noose; she'd seen Goody's torture and hanging. Andrew deserted her, and she was desperate to live. Oh, her baby. She miscarried, Mike. She miscarried in the jail, and no one helped her. They used the baby's horrible demise as evidence against her. Can you imagine?"

Mike's face paled, his eyes filled with confusion and fear. He pulled me close, his arms around me. "You don't know any of that, Sophia. You can't be sure. It was just a dream."

"No, it wasn't!" I whispered, my voice breaking. "She's really out there, bound by darkness, forced to do these terrible things! We must do something. We must call Lee and Matilda back. They know more about this. They might be able to help us."

Mike hesitated; his face torn. "I don't know, Sophia. Lee and Matilda...they're steeped in all this religious stuff. What if bringing them back only makes things worse? What if it provokes Mary somehow? I'm afraid of what might happen if we meddle with things we don't understand."

I looked into his eyes, seeing his fear, understanding his reluctance. But we had no choice. "Mike, I'm scared too. More scared than I've ever been. But we can't just do nothing. We can't just hope it goes away. It hasn't gone away! Mary's soul is in torment, and she's threatening our daughter. We need help. We need Lee and Matilda. I'm not saying we need to call the Catholic Church or a demonologist, but we need help! We are fighting forces we don't understand!"

As if to emphasize my point, our bedroom door slammed shut and shook the entire house. I clutched Mike, and we stared at the door waiting for something else to happen. Besides a few seconds of vicious whispering, nothing else did.

Mike breathed a sigh of relief, running his hands through his hair, his face etched with worry. "Okay. Okay, Sophia. I know you're right. It's hard to accept all this supernatural stuff; I've always been a skeptic, a rational thinker. You know that, but now...now I don't know what to believe."

"We don't have the luxury of disbelief anymore, Mike," I said softly, taking his hand. "We've seen too much, experienced too much. We need to face this, to fight it, with everything we have."

He looked at me, his eyes filled with love and determination. "Okay, Sophia. We'll call them. We'll bring them back. I trust you, and I'll support you. Whatever it takes to keep our family safe." I hugged him, feeling a weight lift from my shoulders. We were in this together, united by love, by fear, by determination. Not like Mary and Andrew. Not like them at all. We would face the darkness, and we would find a way through. Together.

I closed my eyes, leaning into him, feeling a glimmer of hope amid the darkness. We were not alone. We had each other, and we had friends who could help.

The next morning, Mike grabbed his phone, dialing Lee's number, his voice steady as he explained what had happened. I told Lee about the dream and what I'd seen. He didn't question any of it. I could hear the concern in his voice and was relieved to hear his promise to return as soon as possible.

We spent the rest of the next day in a state of tense vigilance, watching over Evie, jumping at every shadow, every creak of the old house. Night fell, and with it came a sense of foreboding, the memories of the nightmare looming large.

Matilda and Lee arrived late, their faces drawn with worry. We sat around the kitchen table, cups of tea growing cold as we shared what had happened.

"Lee filled me in on your dream. Wow. That's a sad turn of events," Matilda said, her voice calm but her eyes sharp. "Mary's transformation, her pact, the souls she needs—these are all pieces of a terrible puzzle. It explains so much. It explains why an innocent child like Elizabeth Kelly would be tormenting Evie. She's under the control of you-know-who."

"And we need to figure out how to break his hold on them all before it's too late," Lee added, his hand on mine, his touch a reassurance. "We'll find a way to save Mary, to protect Evie, to protect all of you."

I looked around the table, at the faces of those I loved and those I trusted. We were in this together, a team united by purpose, by fear, by hope.

"I don't know if we can help Mary. She'd made her choice while she was alive." It was a sad thing to say, but I know what I saw. I couldn't say I blamed her. Mary was sick and frail and half out of her head, but still...why would she agree to that?

"What if she never died, Sophia?" Lee asked seriously. "What then?"

Mike snorted at that suggestion. "Come on, dude. Are you saying Mary Sanford never died? That would make her what? Three hundred years old? If not older? Give me a break. Spirits, maybe I'll believe. Undead witches? I draw the line there."

I took a deep breath, trying to steady myself as I recalled the vivid details of the nightmare. The room was silent, the air thick with tension as everyone waited for me to finish speaking. I hoped by my resharing the details, we could pluck out more hints as to how to defeat the shadow man and Mary Sanford.

"Mary isn't Mary anymore, whether she's dead or alive. The loving, living person she was had long ago left. She's a slave to the darkness, under an eternal pact," Lee said, his voice sad and hopeless.

"A promise, a bond. The devil she dealt with said she would owe him, and when the time came, she would pay," I explained, tears welling in my eyes. "Mary was terrified; she didn't want to die. She made the deal, but she didn't know what it meant. The shadow man never said he wanted her soul, but he wanted something. Something dark and terrible."

I looked at Matilda, her face pale but her eyes filled with understanding. I continued, "Mary came back here, looking for her husband Andrew. But instead, she found us and whoever was here before us. She must have tormented them too. The shadow man told her she must offer up souls to him. That's why she's after Evie, after me. She's bound to him, a slave to his darkness."

The room was silent, the weight of my words settling over us like a dark cloud. Matilda's face was grave, her eyes distant as she considered what I had said.

"This is more serious than we thought," she finally said, her voice measured. "The shadow man, this dark lord, he's the key to all of this. He's the one controlling Mary, driving her to do these terrible things. We need to find out who he is, what he wants."

Mike snorted. "I think we can guess who he is, can't we?"

"Maybe, but let's not assume anything. We need to find a way to break the bond between him and Mary," Lee added, determination in his eyes. "We need to save her, to free her from his grasp. That will end it all."

"You keep saying that, but how?" Mike asked, his voice filled with fear and frustration. "How do we fight something like this? How do we protect our family from something we don't even understand? That's why we invited you back. Sophia and I are not churchgoers. We are certainly not exorcists."

"We'll find a way," Matilda said, her voice firm, her eyes meeting each of ours in turn. "We have to. We have no other choice. This is a battle for Mary's soul, for your family, for everything you hold dear. We will not lose. We cannot lose."

Her words were a rallying cry, a spark of hope in the darkness that surrounded us. We were united, a team driven by love, by fear, by a determination to face the unimaginable and triumph over it. Together, we would face the shadow man, we would face Mary's torment, we would face the darkness.

The room grew colder as we continued our discussion, a tangible sign of the spirits' reaction to our plans. The air seemed to crackle with energy, a mixture of anticipation, anger, and fear. Matilda's eyes widened as she sensed the presence of unseen entities.

"The spirits are restless," she murmured, her voice filled with awe. "They sense what we're doing. Some are angry, some are afraid. But they're all watching us." We looked at each other, a shared understanding passing between us. The spirits were part of this too, their fate tied to ours, to Mary's. We were all in this together.

"We'll come back tonight," Lee said, his voice firm. "We'll bring everything we need to banish Mary Sanford, to break her bond with the shadow man."

"I'll call my mother-in-law and arrange for the kids to be gone," I said, determination in my voice. "We can't risk having them here."

At that, we broke off our meeting, and I set about packing the children's bags. They were happy to go. I kissed them all and hugged them, hoping that this would be over soon.

Mike drove the kids over to his mother's, leaving me alone in the house. The silence was eerie, the atmosphere heavy with the weight of what lay ahead. I wandered into Evie's room, drawn to the evil Stuffy sitting on her bed. How in God's name did he get in here again? The stuffed animal's eyes seemed to glow, a malevolent intelligence lurking within. A chill ran down my spine as I realized that it was watching me, waiting.

I backed out of the room, my heart pounding, my mind a whirl of fear and confusion. This was real, all too real. The evil was here, in our home, in our lives. And we were about to face it head on.

That night, as Mike returned, we stayed together in the living room, the air thick with determination and apprehension. Heavy footsteps stomped above us. The chandelier in the dining room resumed its horrible dance. I heard the whispering, and worst of all, I heard a baby crying. Seeing Mike's face, I knew he could hear it too.

"It's not her, Sophia. It's not our daughter. Don't believe the lie." Mike held me and together we sobbed, but it wasn't a sign that we were quitting. We were setting our grief free. Setting our baby free. Let the crying continue if that's how the devil wanted to play it. He would never turn me against my husband or my children.

He would never make me agree to any kind of deal.

Mike and I looked into each other's eyes. In Mike's I could see an understandable mix of fear and resolve. I did my best to reflect that back to him.

We were ready. We had to be. The shadow man, Mary Sanford, the evil Stuffy—they were all waiting to pounce.

Let them come.

We would face them, together.

Chapter Fifteen—Sophia

I watched as Lee and Matilda began their preparations, unloading strange tools and objects, each with its own purpose in the coming ritual. There was a seriousness in their eyes that sent shivers down my spine. This was real. There was no turning back.

"Salt lines at every door," Lee instructed, his voice firm. "It'll keep the devil from entering the house while we battle Mary. This is a fight not just against her but against the demonic forces that manipulate her."

Matilda reached for the blessed jar of salt and began to carefully line the thresholds of each door. It seemed strange that something as simple as salt could have such power.

"Accusing her is going to be part of this," Matilda explained, her eyes never leaving her work. "Mary's trapped in her own guilt and anger. We need to confront her with the truth, force her to see it. Accusing a witch disables her."

I swallowed hard. The idea of facing that malevolent spirit, accusing her, felt terrifying and intimate all at once.

Lee lit a bundle of white sage, letting it burn and smolder. The pungent scent filled the room, making my head spin slightly. It was like stepping into another world.

"What's the sage for?" Mike asked, looking puzzled.

"To make this space uncomfortable for Mary," Lee answered. "She's still connected to her old self, to her human emotions.

Some part of her will be repelled by the sage. It's a small advantage, but we need everything we can get."

Mike smiled at Lee. "What if she's alive, Lee? What if she's not a spirit? Do you think she's still a three-hundred-year-old witch?"

"Either way, it'll help," Lee said with determination. What was up with Mike being so confrontational? I touched his shoulder. He was tense, as tense as I'd ever seen him.

"Hey, it's going to be okay, honey."

As they continued their preparations, I could feel the atmosphere in the house changing. There was a tension, a weight in the air, like the calm before a storm. My heart raced, and my hands shook as I helped place candles in a circle.

We were about to summon a witch, accuse her, and fight her in a battle that went beyond the physical. The very thought was enough to make my knees weak.

"You sure about this, Sophia?" Mike's voice pulled me back, and I met his concerned eyes.

"I'm scared shitless, but yes, I am sure. Aren't you, honey?" I asked, my voice barely above a whisper. Even if he wasn't, I wanted him to lie to me. I needed a good lie to bolster my confidence.

"Yes, this is what we have to do," he said, wrapping his arms around me. "We have to fight, but I am fighting for the children, and you."

I nodded, knowing he was right. There was no other way. The room was ready, the salt was in place, the sage burning, the candles glowing. We all stood in a circle; our faces lit by flickering shadows.

"It's time," Lee said, his voice resolute. I took a deep breath and looked around at our friends, at the two brave souls who had come to help us. We were ready to face the witch, to accuse her, to battle her. And we would win, no matter what it took.

My hands clenched into fists, determination settling in my chest. Mary Sanford would not defeat us. The ritual began. Lee held an old, weathered book, his eyes scanning the ancient text. "Gather close, and listen well," he instructed us, his voice filled with reverence. We did as he said, the burning sage encircled us, the smell enveloping us, filling the room with a mystical ambiance.

In nomine Patris, et Filii, et Spiritus Sancti, Amen," Lee began, his voice steady and strong. "We stand here, united in purpose, to confront and banish the dark forces that have taken hold in this place. Let no evil pass into our circle, let no malevolence harm us. May the righteous power of the divine protect us and guide us."

A cold shiver ran down my spine as Lee continued to read from the book, the words echoing in the room, heavy with meaning and power.

Something nagged at the edge of my awareness, a strange sensation that grew with every passing second. My eyes darted around the room, searching for the source of the unease.

That's when I saw it. Stuffy.

The evil toy sat on the bookshelf on the other side of the room, its demonic eyes seeming to glow in the dim light. How did it get in here? I clearly saw it upstairs earlier. No matter how many times I put it in the attic or the garbage can, it returned to the house.

"Oh God! Look, Mike!" My heart stopped in my chest as I watched the stuffed animal twitch, a slight but undeniable motion. Until I spoke, everyone's focus had been on Lee and the prayer. I should have kept my mouth shut. I should not have interrupted the prayer, but this turn of events was terrifying and unexpected.

But I knew. I could feel it.

The connection between the demon and Stuffy was growing stronger, and I understood, with terrible clarity, that it was a conduit for the dark force we were trying to banish. "I have to destroy it," I whispered, more to myself than anyone else.

"What?" Mike turned to me with concern in his eyes.

"Stuffy," I said, pointing. "It's connected to the demon. I have to destroy it."

Mike's eyes widened as he followed my gaze, realization dawning on him. Without waiting for a response, I dashed out of the circle and grabbed Stuffy, my hands shaking as I felt the evil that emanated from it.

"Stay in the circle! Sophia!" Matilda warned, but I was already moving toward the fireplace. With a scream of determination, I hurled Stuffy into the flames. The instant the stuffed creature hit the fire, it let out an inhuman wail, a sound so chilling that it froze me in place.

Its eyes glowed a malevolent red, and to my horror, it began to pull itself out of the fire, its body charred and burning but still moving, trying to walk around.

"What is that thing?" Lee cried, his face pale.

"The demon!" I shouted. "It's attached to it."

"But if you burn it, it will be loose!" Lee warned, but it was too late. The room erupted into chaos; the ritual forgotten as we faced the abomination before us.

Stuffy was burning in front of the once-cheerful fireplace, and the demon was breaking free. And it was angry. Mike's face went as white as a ghost as he saw Stuffy walking, still ablaze, still alive. The room was filled with the terrifying wailing, the demonic eyes glowing bright red. Stuffy let out an inhuman scream, one that I prayed I would never hear again.

"Mike, the ax!" I screamed, my voice breaking.

Without hesitation, he grabbed the ax from the wall, his hands sure, his eyes focused. The abomination that was once Stuffy was now crawling towards us, a nightmare come to life. The once-innocent toy now a monstrosity, charred, burning, and alive with malevolent intent.

"Get back!" Mike yelled, raising the ax high. With a series of powerful, determined strikes, he hacked Stuffy to pieces. The room filled with the terrible sounds of cracking and splintering, each blow releasing an otherworldly scream from the demonic toy.

"It's done," Mike said, panting, looking down at the remains of the once-cheerful stuffed animal, now a pile of charred, twisted fabric and stuffing.

But we all felt it.

The room shook, a low rumble that seemed to come from the very walls themselves. The temperature dropped, and shadows played tricks on the walls, forming shapes and figures that weren't there. A chilling wind blew through the room, though the windows were tightly closed.

"What's happening?" Matilda's voice trembled as she clung to Lee. They were the only two still in the circle. Mike and I raced back, but I had no idea if it would protect us at all anymore.

"The demon," Lee said, his face pale, his voice barely above a whisper. "It's loose in the house."

We looked at each other, terror in our eyes. Mike and I had believed that destroying Stuffy would end the nightmare, but we had only unleashed something far more terrifying. Voices whispered in the corners of the room, unintelligible but filled with malice. The air grew heavy, the sense of evil palpable.

"It's here," I whispered, feeling its presence, a dark, cold force that seemed to seep into my very soul. "The demon is here."

"We have to continue the ritual," Lee said, his voice filled with urgency. "Don't leave the circle again! We have to banish it before it gains more power."

"But how?" Matilda's eyes were wide with fear. "It's free. It's in the house. How do we fight it?"

"We fight it together," Mike said, his voice filled with determination. "We stand united, and we fight. We banish this evil, no matter what it takes."

We looked at each other, fear in our eyes but resolve in our hearts. The demon was loose, the battle had only just begun, but we would face it. We would fight it. We would win.

The room continued to shake, the very foundations of the house seeming to tremble with the force of the unleashed demon. Shadows twisted and writhed on the walls, forming faces and figures that seemed to leer at us, taunting us with their malevolence.

Voices were whispering in a language I couldn't understand, their tones dripping with hatred and contempt. The temperature continued to drop, the cold seeping into my bones, a physical manifestation of the evil that now roamed our home.

Suddenly, the wind howled, a sound like a thousand tortured souls, and with a crash, the front door blew open. I turned, my heart in my throat, and there she stood.

Mary Sanford!

She was dressed all in black, in a gown that seemed to consume the light, her face covered by a sheer veil that gave her an otherworldly quality. Her eyes, visible through the veil, were filled with an intensity that seemed to pierce my very soul.

"Andrew," she screamed, her voice carrying across the room, filled with longing and accusation. "Andrew, why did you betray me?"

Mike, still holding the ax, took a step back, his face filled with horror and confusion. "I'm not Andrew," he stammered, his voice trembling. "I am not the one you seek! Leave here, Mary Sanford! This is my house!"

"Don't leave the circle, Mike!" I warned him as I clung to him. But Mary continued to advance, her hands reaching out, her voice filled with pain and anger. "You promised me, Andrew! You promised to love me, to protect me. And then you betrayed me!"

"I didn't betray you," Mike said, his voice stronger now, but there was something in his eyes, a strange attraction, a connection to this spectral figure before us. "I don't know who you think I am, but I'm not Andrew. I'm Mike."

"LIAR!" Mary's voice became a shriek, her face contorted with rage. "You left me to die! You left me to the wolves, to the mob! You promised, Andrew, you promised!"

The room seemed to shake with her anger, the shadows growing darker, the whispers louder. I reached for Mike, my hands shaking, terror washing over me. This wasn't just a confrontation with a ghost. This was something more, something terrifying and dangerous.

"Mike, don't listen to her!" I cried, pulling him back. "She's confused. She's angry. She doesn't know what she's saying."

But Mary's eyes locked onto Mike's, making a connection that seemed to transcend time and space, a bond that was both intimate and horrifying.

"You know me, Andrew," she whispered, her voice soft now, seductive. "You know what we had. You know what you did. I saw what you did, what you did to yourself to escape me. But here you are again, my love. Here you are. Are you ready to make amends for your sins?"

I could see Mike's resolve wavering, the terror in his eyes replaced by something else, something deeper. "Mary?" It was as if he were being drawn to her, pulled by some unseen force. Was she insinuating that Mike used to be Andrew Sanford?

"Mike, fight her! You are not Andrew!" I screamed, my voice desperate. "She's not who you think she is. She's not who she says she is. Fight her, Mike! Fight her!"

But Mary's eyes never left Mike's, her voice a siren song that seemed to call to him, to beckon him closer. "Come to me, Andrew," she whispered, her hands reaching out, her face filled with love and hate, promise and betrayal. "Come to me, and let's finish what we started. We belong together, my love."

Mary's outstretched hands seemed to beg for Mike's touch, her eyes filled with a hunger that went beyond reason. The air was thick with tension, every sound magnified, every shadow a lurking threat. I wept as he moved toward the edge of the circle. "I won't come to you," Mike said finally, his voice filled with resolve, but there was a tremor in his hands, a fear that he couldn't hide.

"You will," Mary's voice was a promise, a threat. "You will come to me, Andrew. You cannot escape what you've done. You cannot escape me!" The room trembled with her anger, her desperation, her need. I could feel it all, a suffocating weight that threatened to crush us.

"Mike, we have to end this," I whispered, my voice trembling. "We have to banish her."

He nodded, his face pale, his eyes haunted. "I know." But he couldn't look away from her. Something was happening between them, but what? What was going on?

Lee and Matilda were ready, their faces determined, their tools in hand. We knew what we had to do. We had to accuse her, to confront her with the truth, to force her to see what she had become.

"Mary Sanford," Lee's voice rang out, clear and strong. "We accuse you of consorting with the devil, of making a pact with evil. You have allowed your anger and your pain to consume you, to turn you into something dark and twisted. We demand that you face the truth, that you see what you have done."

Mary's scream was a sound of pure rage, a sound that chilled my blood. "LIARS! TRAITORS! You know nothing!"

"We know the truth, Mary," Matilda's voice was calm, but there was steel in her eyes. "And we will make you see it. We will make you understand. I accuse you!"

"You cannot make me do anything!" Mary's voice was a snarl, her face a mask of fury. "I am beyond your reach. I am beyond your understanding! I am beyond your control!" She began to laugh madly and uncontrollably.

"No, Mary," I said, stepping in front of Mike, my voice filled with a strength I didn't know I possessed. "You are lost, you are confused, but you are not beyond our reach. You are not beyond redemption. You can still choose to let go of the anger, the hatred. You can choose to be free. I, Sophia, accuse you of witchcraft!"

Mary's laugh was a sound of pure malice. "Free? I am already free." Her voice shifted as she spoke. One moment she sounded like a woman, and the next, she sounded like a beast. "I am free to take what I want, to do what I want. I am free to take my revenge. Andrew! Come with me, and I'll leave these others alone. For now!"

"No, Mary," I said, my voice unwavering. "You cannot have Mike. He is not Andrew! Andrew died a long time ago! Please, Mary! You are trapped. Trapped by your own choices, by your own darkness. We can set you free."

"No!" She screamed in an inhuman voice. The room shook with her anger, the wind howling, the shadows dancing. But we stood firm, united in our purpose, united in our determination to face evil, to fight it, to defeat it.

"We will set you free," I repeated, my voice a promise, a vow. "We can set you free."

The battle had begun.

As her veil blew back, Mary's face twisted into something wickedly beautiful, her eyes sparkling with a dark allure that was impossible to resist. She reached out to Mike, her voice dripping with sweetness, her words a seductive whisper.

"Come to me, Andrew. Come to me and make amends for what you've done. You owe me. You know you do."

I could see Mike's body sway towards her, his eyes locked onto hers, a strange light in them. Fear gripped my heart as I realized what was happening. She was pulling him in, using her power, her charm to draw him to her.

"No!" I screamed, grabbing his hand, and pulling him back, breaking the connection. "Don't listen to her, Mike! She's not who she says she is!"

"But I know her," Mike whispered, his voice filled with confusion, pain. "I know her, and I...I owe her."

"You owe her nothing!" I shouted, my voice filled with desperation. "She's lying to you, confusing you. You must fight it, Mike. You must fight her!"

"I...I..." Mike's voice trailed off, his eyes wide with terror as he looked at Mary, really looked at her. The illusion was beginning to crack, the facade starting to crumble. Lee, Matilda, and I began shouting our accusations.

"Mary Sanford, we accuse you of witchcraft! You stand accused!"

"Look at yourself, Mary!" Matilda commanded, holding up a mirror, forcing Mary to see her reflection, to see what she had become. I hadn't seen the mirror earlier. "Look at what you've done, what you've become. You are not the victim here. You are a perpetrator, a villain. You've chosen this path, and you must face the consequences."

"No!" Mary's voice was a shriek, her face contorting with rage. "You don't understand! You don't know what he did to me! What Andrew took from me!"

"Mary Sanford, we condemn you for witchcraft!" Lee yelled again, his voice filled with authority. "Your power is broken here. You have no hold over us, no control. We see you for what you are, and we reject you!"

"We reject you!" we all echoed, our voices united, our determination unwavering.

Finally, Mike added his voice. He shouted at the top of his lungs. "Mary Sanford, I accuse you of witchcraft!"

Mary's scream was a sound of pure agony, a sound that tore at my soul. But we stood firm, our circle unbroken, our resolve unshaken.

"You cannot defeat me!" Mary's voice was a growl, her eyes wild with fury. "You cannot break me! I will have my revenge!"

"No, Mary," I said, my voice calm, my heart steady. "You will not have your revenge. You will not have anything. Your power is broken here, and we will send you back to where you came from. You will not harm us. You will not harm anyone ever again."

Mary's now-glowing eyes blazed with anger, the mirror reflecting a tortured soul consumed by darkness. "Andrew, why did you forsake me? Why?" she cried, her voice a mixture of pain and fury. She reached out again towards Mike, her hands ghostly pale.

I grabbed Mike's hand, pulling him away from Mary's reach, my heart pounding in my chest. "Mike, don't listen to her!" I screamed.

Matilda quickly held up the mirror to Mary, forcing her to look at herself.

"We must all do it together," Lee shouted over the howling wind. "Mary Sanford, we condemn you for witchcraft! Your power is broken here! Everyone! Say it with me!"

We began to chant the accusation, our voices louder and louder. As we chanted in unison, Mary let out a scream that rattled the very foundation of the house. The mirrors vibrated, the candles flickered, and the temperature dropped further, leaving a thin layer of frost on the windows.

"No!" Mary shrieked. "You cannot banish me so easily. I will return, and vengeance will be mine. Andrew, you will understand the depth of my pain!" With a final wail, she vanished into the night, leaving us standing in stunned silence. The wind died down, and the door slammed shut with a loud bang.

We stood there, our breath visible in the chilly air, feeling the weight of what had just happened. The demon was loose, Mary had been confronted but not defeated, and Mike...Mike was changed. His face was pale, his eyes distant, and he kept muttering Andrew's name.

"It's not over," Matilda said quietly, her voice heavy with dread. "She will return, and we must be ready."

"But how?" I whispered, feeling a chill that had nothing to do with the temperature. "What more can we do?"

"We'll find a way," Lee assured us, but there was uncertainty in his eyes. "We must."

As we began to clean up, a strange noise echoed through the house, like distant laughter, malevolent and cold. I looked around, my skin crawling, but saw nothing. Yet, the sound lingered, a haunting reminder that Mary's threat was far from empty. The battle was won, but the war was far from over. Mary Sanford was still out there, and something told me that the worst was yet to come.

I glanced at Mike, who was still lost in thought, and a shiver ran down my spine. Whatever connection he had to Mary, to Andrew, it was a link that could be our salvation or our downfall. The house settled into an eerie silence, but the echo of Mary's words lingered in the air, and the sinister laughter seemed to resonate in the very walls.

The game had changed, the stakes were higher, and the terror was only just beginning.

Lee turned to the three of us. "Take a break. Get some water, go to the bathroom, but everyone stay together. We must reset the circle and get ready. That was just the first round."

"The first round?" I asked, trying not to sound so hopeless.

Lee nodded glumly. Mike headed to the kitchen to grab bottles of water, and I trailed behind him. For the first time in a long time, I prayed.

Prayed that God would stand with us.

Chapter Sixteen—Sophia

We'd barely returned to the living room and cracked open the water bottles when the laughter started again. Mary's mad laughter bounced off the walls and the electricity flickered off and on.

Matilda began muttering incantations, holding up holy symbols that seemed to glow with divine light. But Mary was relentless, her fury a palpable force that seemed to tear at the very fabric of reality. The room became a chaotic swirl of shadows and whispers, the temperature dropping so suddenly that my breath fogged in the air. I could feel the demonic presence lurking, waiting, its malevolence a dark undercurrent to Mary's wrath. It was outside the house but how long would those salt lines hold? I had no idea.

"Andrew!" Mary's voice was a siren call, seductive and terrifying. Mary was back and standing in front of the bookshelf where Stuffy once sat. She reached out, her hands ghostly claws, her eyes fixed on Mike. Mary floated a few inches above the floor and sailed toward us. "Why did you betray me? Why?"

Mike's face was pale, his eyes wide with horror and confusion. He seemed drawn to her, pulled by some unseen force. I tightened my grip on his hand, pulling him back, away from the beautiful but deadly specter.

"We must do more!" Matilda cried, her voice edged with desperation. "She's too strong! Lee! We need to find another way!" I could see the fear in her eyes, the realization that our preparations, our rituals, were not enough. Mary's ghost was more powerful than we had anticipated, her connection to the demon amplifying her strength.

"Keep fighting!" Lee urged, his voice cracking with strain. "We can't let her win! We must banish her, break her connection to this world!"

We tried everything, throwing salt, reciting prayers, holding up mirrors and crosses. We accused again and again, but nothing seemed to break her power. Mary's presence was relentless, her verbal attacks growing more ferocious, her words more poisonous. One moment she was seducing Mike, and the next, she was bombarding Andrew with a flurry of disgusting slurs. Then it got personal.

"You never wanted that baby, Sophia. Does he know? Does he know about your drinking? Oh, thou art an evil woman, Sophia!"

I wept at her words. "She's lying, Mike! I never did that! I never drank while I was pregnant!"

"I know, honey! She's a demon! Curse you, Mary Sanford!"

Mary's answer was to continue to laugh maniacally. She knew us, knew our fears, our weaknesses, and she used them against us. "You cannot defeat me," she hissed, her voice dripping with malice. "I will not be denied! I will not be silenced! Andrew is mine!"

Her eyes locked onto mine, and for a terrifying moment, I felt her inside my mind, her anger, her pain, her madness. It was overwhelming, a tidal wave that threatened to pull me under.

It made me drop to my knees. I screamed, my voice lost in the cacophony of the battle. We were losing, and I knew it. Desperation clawed at my throat, panic rising like a tide.

"Mike isn't Andrew! He is not yours!"

She screamed in anger, but she wasn't going to relent. Mike appeared to be growing weaker by the moment too.

"We need to find another way!" I cried out, hoping either Matilda or Lee would hear me. My voice was hoarse. "We are losing! We can't beat her like this!"

The room was a whirlwind of terror and confusion as the battle with Mary became a maelstrom that seemed to have no end. We were trapped, caught in a fight we couldn't win. And I knew, with a terrible certainty, that if we didn't find a way to stop her, we would all be lost.

The battle with Mary's ghost raged on, a whirlwind of spectral attacks and desperate defenses. But as the minutes dragged into what felt like hours, something began to change within me. I could feel a connection to Mary growing, a thread of understanding that reached beyond the anger and terror.

Her pain, her anger, her sense of betrayal—it resonated with something deep inside me.

I could feel her agony, and it was both terrifying and strangely compelling.

"Mary!" I shouted, my voice breaking through the chaos. "I know your pain! I understand what you feel, but this is wrong! You know it is wrong! Fight him, Mary! Fight him!"

The room fell silent for a moment. Mary's ghostly figure paused, her dark eyes fixed on me. It was a look of recognition, of shared sorrow.

"You can't understand!" she wailed; her voice filled with anguish. "You can't know what he did to me! What they all did!"

"But I do!" I insisted, tears streaming down my face. "I know betrayal, I know hurt! The baby! You wanted the baby! You never wanted to lose her. It was a little girl, Mary. You lost a little girl, like I did. Let us help you! Let us heal you!"

Her face twisted, torn between rage and longing. I could feel her struggle, the part of her that wanted to lash out, and the part that wanted to be free.

"We can help you find peace, Mary," I shouted, reaching out to her. "Trust me. Let me help you. I know your pain!"

But even as I spoke, I could feel the dark presence lurking, watching, feeding off the negative energy. The demon was still here, still influencing events, and it was growing stronger by the moment.

The temperature dropped further, shadows twisting into malevolent shapes, whispers growing louder, more insistent. There was a smell of brimstone in the air, a tangible sense of evil.

"No!" Mary screamed; her voice filled with panic. "He won't let me go! He won't set me free! It hurts me! He hurts me!"

And just like that, the connection between us snapped, her anger and fear overwhelming everything else. She attacked again, her spectral force more ferocious than ever, driven by the demon's insidious influence.

"Mary! Fight him! You can't surrender!" Lee shouted, his face pale. "It's feeding off her, off all of us! We need to break its hold!"

But how? The demon was a shadow, a whisper, an intangible force that seemed to permeate everything. He refused to manifest and remained hidden. We were trapped in a battle with an enemy we couldn't see or touch, and it was winning.

The room shook, the very walls seeming to tremble as the demon's power grew. It was becoming more real, more substantial, its influence spreading like a dark stain.

"We're running out of time!" Matilda cried; her face etched with fear. "We need to do something, now!" But what? What could we do? The demon was everywhere and nowhere, a phantom that defied all our efforts to fight it.

Desperation settled in, a cold, heavy weight that threatened to crush us. We were losing, and I knew that if we didn't find a way to stop the demon, to free Mary from its clutches, we would all be lost.

The battle raged on, the stakes higher than ever, the danger growing with every passing second. We were in a fight for our very souls, and I had no idea how we were going to win. Mike's eyes glazed over, his expression changing, his body posture shifting. He began to speak, but his voice was different, the words coming out in an old dialect, a language from another time.

"Mary," he said, his voice filled with sorrow and regret. "Mary, 'tis I, Andrew. I failed thee, dear wife. I let thee down and allowed fear and suspicion to cloud my judgment. I believed them over thee, and now I see the error of my ways."

The room went silent, everyone was staring at Mike in shock. But I knew it was no longer just Mike speaking; it was Andrew, Mary's betrayer husband, reaching out through time and space. Andrew was here, and he was trying to make things right.

My heart sank down to my shoes. I didn't want this to happen, but I knew it needed to.

"Canst thou ever forgive me, my love?" Mike continued, tears in his eyes. "I wronged thee so grievously. I beg thy forgiveness. Mary, I love thee. I have always loved thee."

Mary's figure trembled, her eyes widening as she looked at Mike. Her face was a mask of shock, confusion, and then, slowly, recognition. For the first time since I'd encountered the spirit of Mary Sanford, she smiled, and it was a hopeful thing.

"Andrew?" she whispered, her voice trembling. "Is it truly thee?"

"It is I, Mary," Mike replied, his voice gentle, loving. Without a word, he left the circle, left safety behind. But it wasn't Mike anymore. This was Andrew Sanford, come home to his wife, to his greatest failure and sin.

"I have come to make amends, to heal thy wound, a wound that I have caused thee." He reached out, and though she was a specter, he seemed to take her in his arms. The demon screamed somewhere outside, a sound of pure rage and frustration that shook the very foundations of the house.

"You must heal her, Andrew!" Matilda shouted to Mike, her voice filled with determination. "It's the only way to defeat the demon. We must break her bond with the shadow man."

The room was filled with a golden light, a warmth that seemed to permeate everything. Andrew and Mary were locked in an embrace, their forms merging, becoming one. My heart sank at the sight.

Oh please, God. Don't take Mike from me. Don't make him pay for Andrew's crimes!

"Wife, I long for thee. I long for thy forgiveness. I failed thee in life, but I shall not fail thee in death. For wherever you go, there shall I go too. Say you forgive me, Mary."

Mary began to cry. "I forgive thee, Andrew," she said, her voice filled with love and understanding. "I forgive thee for all thy deeds."

The demon's scream turned into a wail of defeat, a sound of pure despair. The shadows retreated, the whispers faded to silence, and the temperature slowly returned to normal.

The golden light grew brighter, surrounding Andrew and Mary, healing the wounds of the past and breaking the bonds that had held them. Yes, Mike appeared different somehow. Taller, with long hair and a slender look to his face.

Where was my husband? Was I going to lose him forever? "Mike?" I whispered tearfully.

"Andrew did it," Lee whispered, his voice filled with awe. "He has healed her. The demon is defeated, for he cannot stand in the face of forgiveness."

The light faded, leaving the room as it had been, but with a sense of peace, a feeling of resolution. Mary's image vanished into a hundred balls of golden light. Each ball rose to the ceiling and disappeared. Mike collapsed on the floor, his body wracked with sobs, but they were tears of relief, of redemption. "Mike! Baby! Oh my God! Mike are you okay?" I raced to his side and held him as he sobbed.

We had won. Somehow, we had won! We faced the demon, faced our fears, and we emerged victorious. Mary was free, her soul at peace and her love for Andrew restored.

For a moment, the room was filled with a palpable sense of relief. Mike, his face streaked with tears, looked around, breathing heavily. Matilda and Lee were exchanging smiles, their expressions showing the weight of the moment. We all felt it—the freedom, the release, the peace.

"I can't believe we did it," I murmured, my eyes glistening with unshed tears.

"It's over," Lee said, letting out a sigh of relief. "Mary is finally at peace. She's free!"

Just as the weight of their accomplishment began to sink in, the house suddenly rumbled, causing the chandelier above to sway ominously. The shadows, which had earlier receded, began to gather once more, this time more pronounced, more threatening.

"What...what's happening?" Matilda stammered, her eyes darting around the room.

A cold, sinister laugh echoed through the room, sending shivers down everyone's spines. The windows frosted over, and the temperature dropped rapidly.

"It seems we're not done after all," Lee muttered, his face turning ashen.

The demon's voice, guttural and dripping with malice, resonated throughout the house.

"You may have freed her, but I am still here. And now, you have my undivided attention."

The room darkened further as the laugh grew louder, the atmosphere heavy with the promise of a more significant challenge. The demon was still at large, and it was clear that our battle was far from over.

I clutched Mike's arm, my face filled with dread. "What have we unleashed?"

The morning sun barely penetrated the heavy atmosphere of the house. It had been a long night, but this wasn't over yet. Mike looked drained after channeling Andrew. The smell of sage, now mingled with brimstone, lingered in the air.

"This is our turf," Lee announced, his voice firm, "and we'll defend it."

We gathered around the dining table, a chaotic spread of texts, scrolls, and artifacts before us. I felt a tug in my chest as I spoke. "It feeds on our fear, our negative energy. But what does it truly want?"

Matilda's eyes were buried in a worn-out book as she replied, "There's always a deeper motive. Perhaps something or someone here is what it's truly after."

I glanced at Mike, noticing his distant expression, the burden of Andrew's memories haunting him.

"There's a vendetta. A purpose," Mike whispered. "It's getting stronger," he murmured, clutching his head in pain, "the memories, the visions. There's something...something crucial that you don't know. I can't explain it, Sophia, but I was him. I was Andrew Sanford. She was my wife. I can't believe I am saying this."

"Go on, honey," I encouraged him. "Tell us what you know!"

His eyes lost focus, fixed on some unseen horror. "Oh God. A ritual—I remember the ritual," he continued, his voice breaking, "A binding that tied the demon to the Sanford lineage. Mary knew nothing about it, but my father did. He made the deal. He participated in the binding, as did I, Andrew, but I was only a child. I hardly understood it. We need to undo it."

As if on cue, the soft notes of a haunting melody filled the house, drawing us up the staircase like moths to a flame. "Where is that coming from?" I asked no one in particular. Each of us grabbed an item from the table, except Mike, who again opted for the ax. We journeyed up the staircase and toward the attic. Yes, that's where the sound came from.

In the dimly lit attic, amidst relics of the past, an antique music box played, its ballerina twirling to a tune that sent shivers down my spine. Mike swayed as if in a trance, tears brimming in his eyes.

"This...this was her music box," he whispered.

As I reached out to stop the music box, a creaking floorboard caught Lee's attention. We exchanged a glance, our instincts kicking in. Together, we pried it open, revealing a concealed circle etched with ancient symbols hidden beneath. Matilda leaned in, her experienced eyes wide, her fingers delicately tracing the lines of a complicatedly tied cord.

"This is it," she said, her voice trembling with both excitement and fear. "This was used in the binding ritual. Mary led us here! It's the key to breaking the bond. Mary wants this broken, for you, for all of you."

No sooner had the words left her lips than the room plunged into darkness. The barriers that had seemed so solid were now crumbling, the walls groaning as an inhuman whisper filled the room.

"You cannot break what is eternal."

We stood united, but our determination was overshadowed by the terrifying realization of what lay ahead. The true fight was only beginning, and I knew we were facing an evil far more ancient and relentless than we could have imagined. But we pressed on.

The room came alive with resonant, otherworldly energy as Matilda and Lee began to chant, their voices intertwining and reverberating through the air. The concealed circle glowed, a faint, mystical hum emanating from its core. Mike, standing at the center with a silver knife that Lee had given him, looked both determined and vulnerable.

The tension in the room reached a fever pitch. I felt something beyond our world pulling at me, time bending to the ritual's will.

With a trembling hand, Mike cut through the bundle of cords with the silver knife. Doing so, he severed the ethereal connection that I could sense but not see. The room shuddered, a chorus of freed voices rising in a harmonious release.

The glow of the circle slowly faded, leaving us in a silence filled with awe, relief, and the chilling echo of a defeated demon's cry, "No!"

We stood united, victorious, yet aware that the battle was not over. Though we had severed the demon's connection to the spirits and freed them from its grasp, the demon itself remained at large, trapped but unbroken at River Run.

It could no longer torment the family that had built the home, but its malevolence lingered, I couldn't deny that. Even months later, I would sense a dark shadow outside the house. It had not found its way in yet, but it wanted to. It wanted to find its way back in, but I wouldn't allow that to happen. Never. Not as long as I had breath in my body.

The room was still, the lingering echoes of the ritual fading into silence. I looked over at Mike, his face pale but his eyes bright with a mixture of relief, determination, and a spark of triumph. Our gazes locked, and something unspoken passed between us—a recognition of what we had accomplished, the battles we had faced, and the love that had carried us through.

He took my hands in his, his fingers warm and steady. The weariness and terror of the past few hours were still etched on his face, but there was a new strength there too, a confidence forged in the fires of our shared ordeal.

"We did it," he whispered, his voice filled with emotion. "We did it together."

I nodded, tears pricking at my eyes. "We did," I agreed, squeezing his hands. "We faced it, and we won. Together."

He pulled me into his arms, holding me close, his heart beating strong and steady against mine. I buried my face in his chest, letting the warmth and strength of his embrace wash over me. We had faced unimaginable horrors, confronted our deepest fears, and we had come out on the other side, stronger and more united.

"We'll face whatever comes next," Mike murmured, his lips against my hair. "We'll face it together."

I looked up at him, our eyes meeting, our souls connecting in a way that went beyond words. I knew he was right. Whatever lay ahead, we would face it, and we would do it together. We had each other, and that was enough.

In that moment, the looming shadow of the demon, the uncertainty of what lay ahead, all of it faded away. All that mattered was us, our love, and the unbreakable bond that had carried us through the darkest of nights.

We sealed our victory with a kiss, a promise of love and commitment that no demon, no darkness could ever break.

159

Epilogue—Sophia

Life after the haunting took on a new rhythm, a quieter melody that sang of peace and healing. Our home was once filled with terror and uncertainty, and it now resonated with love and the laughter of a family united. The walls no longer whispered of torment; instead, they echoed the joy and triumph of those who had faced the darkness and emerged victorious.

Mike and I grew closer in ways we could never have imagined. We had looked into the abyss, faced our deepest fears, and come out the other side changed, stronger, and more in love. Our nights were no longer plagued by nightmares but by dreams of hope and promise.

Even our little ones seemed to sense the change. They played and giggled with newfound freedom, unburdened by the shadows that had once lingered over our home. One evening, as we gathered in the living room, a gentle breeze danced through the open window, carrying with it a faint melody of a forgotten song. A song from the music box.

The spirits were at peace, their eternal rest finally granted. I felt a warmth, a presence that thanked us and bade us farewell. A final, gentle reminder that we were never alone.

We decided to honor the legacy of Mary Sanford in a special way. A plaque was placed by the ancient oak tree, her unofficial resting place, with words of remembrance and forgiveness. Her story would be remembered not as a tragedy of betrayal and darkness but as a symbol of redemption, love, and the power of understanding.

As the seasons changed and time rolled on, we never forgot what we had experienced, what we had learned. Our home was a sanctuary, a place of love and family, forever touched by a history that had brought us to the brink and back.

And yet, the world is vast, filled with mysteries and unexplored corners that beckon to the curious and the brave. Who knows what adventures await, what secrets lie hidden, waiting to be uncovered?

For now, we bask in the warmth of our triumph, grateful for the lessons, the love, and the unbreakable bonds that have shaped us.

The memory of River Run, of Mary and Andrew, of the demon and the battle, will forever be a part of us, a reminder that light can triumph over darkness, that love can heal even the deepest wounds.

We face the future with open hearts, unafraid and full of hope, knowing that whatever comes our way, we'll face it together.

And in the quiet corners of our home, in the gentle rustle of the leaves and the soft whispers of the wind, the spirits sigh and I hear them.

I suppose I always will.

THE END

Author's Note

Thank you for journeying with me through the haunted halls and storied past of River Run. Writing this novel has been an incredible adventure, one that has challenged me, inspired me, and allowed me to explore themes that are dear to my heart.

River Run was born from a fascination with the witchcraft trials and a desire to delve into the mysteries that lie just beyond our understanding. It's a story about love and family, fear and courage, forgiveness and redemption. In weaving together the threads of history, supernatural elements, and human emotion, I hoped to create a tapestry that resonates with readers on many levels.

I wanted to write a tale that not only thrilled and chilled but also offered a glimpse into the complexities of the human heart. The characters of Sophia, Mike, Mary and Andrew Sanford, and others were my companions on this journey, and I've grown to love them deeply. Their struggles, triumphs, and connections are reflections of our own, reminders that even in the face of darkness, we have the power to choose love, understanding, and hope.

And we have the power to make the wrong choices, and we all often do.

The historical elements of the story, including the portrayal of witch trials and the Puritan era, were inspired by extensive research. While *River Run* is a work of fiction, it pays homage to the very real tragedies and triumphs of our shared history. The legacy of the real Mary Sanford is symbolic of the many voices that have been silenced, misunderstood, or forgotten, and I felt a profound responsibility to honor them in these pages.

A special thanks must be extended to all those who supported me in bringing *River Run* to life. My family, friends, and you, dear reader, have all played a crucial role in this endeavor. Your encouragement, engagement, and passion for storytelling are what make this journey worthwhile.

Lastly, I invite you to reflect on the themes of *River Run* as you go about your daily life. May we all strive to understand and love one another better, face our fears with courage, and embrace the mysteries that make our world so wonderfully complex.

With heartfelt gratitude,

M. L. Bullock

P.S. Feel free to follow me on my Facebook page[1] or visit my author page at MLBullock.com[2].

---

1. http://www.facebook.com/authormlbullock

2. http://www.mlbullock.com

Don't miss out!

Visit the website below and you can sign up to receive emails whenever M.L. Bullock publishes a new book. There's no charge and no obligation.

https://books2read.com/r/B-A-CXMC-IFZMC

BOOKS 2 READ

Connecting independent readers to independent writers.

Also by M.L. Bullock

Create and Prosper
The Prolific Writer: How to Write and Create a Successful
Catalog of Books

Desert Queen Saga
The Tale of Nefret
The Falcon Rises
The Kingdom of Nefertiti
The Song of the Bee Eater

Devecheaux Antiques and Haunted Things Trilogy Series
Devecheaux Antiques and Haunted Things
A Cup of Shadows
A Voice From Her Past
A Watch Of Weeping Angels

Gulf Coast Paranormal
The Ghosts of Kali Oka Road
The Ghosts of the Crescent Theater
A Haunting on Bloodgood Row
The Legend of the Ghost Queen
A Haunting at Dixie House
The Ghost Lights of Forrest Field
The Ghost of Gabrielle Bonet
The Ghost of Harrington Farm
The Creature on Crenshaw Road
A Ghostly Ride in Gulfport
The Ghosts of Phoenix No.7
The Maelstrom of the Leaf Academy
The Ghosts of Oakleigh House
The Spirits of Brady Hall
The Gray Lady of Wilmer

Gulf Coast Paranormal Season Three
Tower of Darkness
Haunted Molly

Gulf Coast Paranormal Season Two
The Wayland Manor Haunting
The Beast of Limerick House
The Beast of Limerick House

A Haunting at Goliath Cave
Death Among the Roses
The Captain of Water Street
Return to the Leaf Academy

Gulf Coast Paranormal Trilogy Series
Ghosted
Haunted
Dead
Spooked
Paranormal

Haunting Passions
For the Love of Shadows
Her Haunted Heart

Idlewood
The Ghosts of Idlewood
Dreams of Idlewood
The Whispering Saint
The Haunted Child

Laurel House
Whispers

Lost Camelot
Guinevere Unconquered
The Undead Queen of Camelot

Lost Camelot Trilogy
Guinevere Forever

Marietta
The Bones of Marietta
Footsteps of Angels

Morgans Rock
The Haunting of Joanna Storm
The Hall of Shadows
The Ghost of Joanna Storm

Return to Seven Sisters
The Roses of Mobile
All the Summer Roses
Blooms Torn Asunder
A Garden of Thorns
Wreath of Roses

River Run
River Run

Scary Fall Stories
Horrible Little Things

Seven Sisters
Seven Sisters
Moonlight Falls On Seven Sisters
Shadows Stir At Seven Sisters
The Stars That Fell
The Stars We Walked Upon
The Sun Rises Over Seven Sisters
Beyond Seven Sister
Ghost on a Swing

Shabby Hearts
A Touch Of Shabby
Shabbier By The Minute
Shabby By Night
Shabby All The Way
Star Spangled Shabby

Southern Gothic
Being With Beau
Death's Last Darling
Spook House

Southland
Southland

Sugar Hill
Wife Of The Left Hand
Fire On The Ramparts
Blood By Candlelight
The Starlight Ball
His Lovely Garden

Summerleigh
The Belles of Desire, Mississippi
The Ghost Of Jeoprady Belle
The Lady In White
Loxley Belle

Supernatural Support Group

Circle of Shadows

The Mummy Queen's Revenge
Queen Mummy

Twelve to Midnight
Mary Twelves

Standalone
The Hauntings of Idlewood
Lost Camelot
The Desert Queen Collection
Haunting Passions
Ghosts on a Plane
Halloween Screams
Dead Is the Loneliest Place to Be
Ghost Story
Believer's Guide to Paranormal Ministry

Watch for more at www.mlbullock.com.

About the Author

Author M.L. Bullock enjoys the laid-back atmosphere and the spooky vibe of the Gulf Coast, especially the region's historic districts and sites. When she isn't visiting her favorite haunts in New Orleans or Old Mobile, you can find her flipping through old photographs or newspaper clippings in search of new inspiration.

Read more at www.mlbullock.com.

www.ingramcontent.com/pod-product-compliance
Lightning Source LLC
Chambersburg PA
CBHW050519160726
48003CB00001B/380